Matt Cairone

This is a work of fiction. Names, characters, places, and incidents either are the product of the author's imagination or are used fictitiously.

Matt Cairone was born in 1958 in Atlantic City, New Jersey. He received a B.A. from Dartmouth College in 1980 and a J.D. from the University of Pittsburgh School of Law in 1984. He entered the practice of law in Michigan in 1984 and moved his practice to Pennsylvania in 1987, where he lives in Canonsburg, outside of Pittsburgh, with his wife, Shannon. In addition to his law practice, he writes fiction and music. He and his wife, Shannon, own American Quarter horses and enjoy traveling and showing across the country.

This book is dedicated to my wife, Shannon, my daughter, Lia, and my son, Charlie.

Chapter 1

The Brit sat down at table fifteen, seat eight. It was the one dollar, three dollar no limit Texas hold'em poker game. None of the other nine players looked up or otherwise acknowledged his arrival. He put his chips on the table in neat, even stacks. He pulled two yellow chips from the pocket of his sport coat and played with them between his fingers.

The Brit gambled for a living. And a painful living it was. He could play the right hands. He could fold the right hands. He could play the right percentages. He could make the right bets. He could read his opponents. But, in the end, it was a card game. And if the right cards were not dealt, he could lose to the rankest of amateurs. Any hand, anytime, anywhere.

The Brit had been playing well, but he had been losing. He normally played in the casinos in his hometown, London. But in the last six weeks he had run into such bad luck that even his wife encouraged him to leave home to try and change his fortune. She would stay and play in London, minding the home front. He was in Las Vegas.

The Brit normally had a goal to win at least $500 over the eighteen or so hours he played each day, every day. That is why he chose a low stakes game, which would be more often than not made up of amateurs. This, however, was a double-edged sword. Amateurs make amateur mistakes. They play hands that they should fold. They get impatient not being in the action. Many of the amateurs come to the low stakes table with money that they can afford to lose. This is a dangerous situation for the professional. The Brit often was upset when a hand was lost that should have been won, but he understood it. He had consciously, knowingly, and deliberately chosen his own poison. He recognized and embraced the subjective nature of his existence. It was simply his everyday life.

The Brit, trying to climb out of the hole he had dug in London, had set an unusually high objective of making at least $1,000 a day in Vegas. His plan was to stay for three nights and four days. He brought with him $10,000 in US cash. He left $9,000 of it in the safe in his room to avoid the temptation of playing and losing too much too soon.

The Brit started slowly. He was trying to learn the "tells" of each of the players. The "tells" in poker are critical; they are the idiosyncratic giveaways that a good player can discern about another player to predict the strength or weakness of that player's hand. The Brit, with knitted brow, studied each of the other nine players intently. Patience, he told himself, sound play and patience.

The Brit had only played one hand in the first hour and a half, winning a small pot by limping into the betting with a hand where everybody was weak and folded early. He felt like he had a reasonably good read on his opponents at the table. He screwed the plastic cap off of the top of his plastic bottle of water and took a deep gulp. He replaced the cap and set the bottle down on the stand beside his chair. He inhaled deeply and exhaled slowly. It was time to start playing. Just give me some cards, he thought.

Now when the Brit plays he plays. He would leave the game only when he was absolutely too tired to stay upright, and then only for a few hours of sleep; time was money, one way or the other. He would leave the table only when he had to use the restroom, and he would try to do that during a dealer switch to not miss any hands. He usually would drink only coffee or water, and he would take whatever amphetamine he had recently procured, as needed, during his visits to the bathroom. All of this made the Brit a very difficult "tell." He was so hopped up on caffeine and uppers that he had more twitches and tics than most players could follow. Trying to figure out his physical mannerisms would be like trying to learn the characters of all three alphabets used in Japanese over the course of three days. The combination of stress and drugs caused his mood to be erratic. At times he was chatty, in his quaint accent, and downright upbeat. This usually occurred sometime shortly after a bathroom break. At other times he was downright depressed, sullen and looked positively ill.

He could get cranky at times. But the anger was always short lived. He knew that a poker player must have a short memory to stay sane. A winning hand is nice, and a losing hand with money in the pot is bad; both are fleeting. New cards are dealt before you can even think about what happened. The game goes on.

After about eight hours of play, the Brit was up only a bit. It was a slow start and a trend he would need to reverse soon.

Hunger struck him for the first time. He did not eat for pleasure or enjoyment; he ate only for the strength necessary to keep him at the table. He called for a menu. He never missed a play or held up the game while he looked it over and ordered.

In about twenty minutes the cocktail waitress came back to the table with the Brit's food. He had ordered a Chinese dish that came in a large plastic container, which he balanced on his legs. He ate deftly with chopsticks, again never missing a hand or holding up the game. He ate like a wolf, looking this way and that to make sure no one was coming for his food or to take advantage of his momentary vulnerability. As soon as he was finished, which was very quickly, he tossed the empty container onto the drink tray behind him and turned back to face the table again, fortified.

"Now I feel better," he said to no one in particular. And no one in particular listened.

It was a new hand. The first card was dealt to all and then the next. The Brit cupped his hands to hide his cards while he looked at them. He had two Queens. This was the third strongest hand before the flop, third obviously only to two Aces or to two Kings. He was in a middle position, and he thought hard to himself about how to bet this reasonably good hand. As the action came to him, he decided to make a small raise. He was hoping to keep as many players in for as long as possible to maximize the pot, which based on the percentages should be his to take. Three other players stayed in the game before the flop. The dealer burnt one card and turned over three; there were a nine of hearts, a three of clubs, and a Queen of diamonds. This was great for the Brit. He had three Queens. There was no flush draw showing, and the straight draw was remote and could be smoked out on another round of betting. The first player checked and the Brit bet $40. Both of the other players called. The pot was growing and he was in good shape. The dealer burnt a card and threw out the turn card. It was a King and the Brit was happy inside, but did not let a shred of emotion show. If someone had pocket Kings he was in trouble, but the chances of that were remote. What he hoped was that another player had one King, and would think that the Brit was playing a pair of Queens. The first player checked and the Brit decided to check too, trying to draw the third player into a big bet with the presumption of a pair of Kings. "I'm all in," said the man at seat 1. The only other player in the game, the one between the Brit and the player all in, contorted his face, fondled his chips, tilted his head this way and that, and finally pushed his cards into the middle, folding. The Brit did not hesitate. "I call," and he flipped over his pocket Queens. "Shit," muttered the man at seat 1. The dealer held up his hand reprimanding the man for the profanity. While he was being admonished, the Brit's opponent turned over two Aces. I've played this right, the Brit thought.

"I only have one out," said the man at seat 1. The dealer burnt a card and turned over the river. The Brit couldn't believe it. He sat up and felt a kick to his gut. It was an Ace.

He saw but did not hear the commotion from the other players at the table, their smiles and expressions of disbelief. How could they be reveling in this gut wrenching loss? He could not be angry with the player at seat 1 for playing the hand, but he could be angry at the preposterous bad luck he was having. And he could be angry at the other players who had no idea what this meant to him and his objectives. This was not a game, this was his livelihood.

The player at seat 1 mouthed to him "Nice hand," with an apologetic, sad face. The Brit was offended. You won you bastard, he thought. "Don't patronize me, mate", he said softly, almost to himself.

The Brit stood up and walked in circles around his chair, pulling at his hair and looking at the ceiling. Ten hours of play, now down $300, and just missing a pot of almost $800. That was the pot he needed to make his nut for the day. It wasn't just being down the $300, which would be a minor problem. It was the loss of a big pot that was, according to the percentages, his to rake in.

He sat out two hands while he composed himself. He remembered his yoga practice. He breathed in slowly and exhaled even more slowly, trying to empty every last breath from his lungs.

Such is life, he thought to himself. He reached into his pocket and pulled out $500. He laid the five bills on the table, and the dealer called out to the boss that a player was buying back in. The new chips arrived, the Brit sat down and refocused, and the game went on.

Chapter 2

At just about the same time the Brit was leaving the table to get a few hours of sleep, which was around 1:00 p.m. Las Vegas time, Dan Berry was kissing his wife goodbye in their kitchen in Bromley, Kentucky. He could see the Ohio River from his back porch. He walked around the house to the car parked on the street. Dan was heading to the Cincinnati airport for the 6:00 afternoon flight to Las Vegas.

He was on his way to the annual meeting and trade show for kitchen and bath dealers. It was a trip he looked forward to, with easy days at the booth and fun nights in the casinos and bars with colleagues he saw only this one time a year. He might even find time to convince a few distributors and fabricators to specify his countertop and tub materials.

Last year Dan brought his wife to the show. They had a good time, but he was secretly happy to be going it alone this year; later nights and more partying. He was a little guilty about feeling this way as he turned the key and started the engine.

Dan pulled onto the street and headed for Interstate 75 South. He flipped on the local sports talk radio and listened to chatter about the Bengals and the upcoming season and the Reds and their playoff chances. The phone cut the radio off.

"Hey, this is Dan Berry," he said as he picked up the call on the hands free.

"Hi Dan, this is David. Listen, I can't make the meeting. Little Davie is sick, and he needs some blood work done and Kathy is uncomfortable with me being so far away."

"I'm sorry to hear that David. Is he alright?"

"We think so, Dan. But thanks. It's more the distance just in case, you know?"

"Yeah, I understand."

"Sorry to leave ya hanging, but you'll be in charge at the booth," he paused to sneeze.

"Bless you" Dan said.

"Thanks," and he sneezed again. "Always twice," and he wiped his nose and went on, "you know we have to keep the booth manned all the time when the show is open, so make sure that's done, ok?"

"No problem, David. You can count on me."

"Thanks, Dan. Stay in touch and let me know about the show and the leads we're getting. And don't kill yourself with the boozing and gambling. Everything in moderation," and after a short pause he continued, "including moderation."

They both laughed.

"Will do, buddy. Sorry you're gonna miss it. Give my best to Kathy and good luck with the little guy. I'm sure he'll be fine."

"Thanks. Have a safe trip. See ya."

Shit, thought Dan. Now I have more responsibility with work and less time for fun. He turned up the radio, switched to a local oldies station, and kept the beat to the music with his fingers on the steering wheel.

The airport was relatively quiet. It was Tuesday afternoon, a slower travel day. Dan checked his bag and headed for the security line. He flew over 150,000 miles a year to peddle polyester and acrylic sheets for use in bath tubs, hot tubs, countertops, and signs. He went everywhere.

The recent economic downturn had been very bad for the business in general and for Dan in particular. His numbers were way off and the plant was now only running one of four production lines. This show was important because things were starting to pick up, and making sure his sales numbers kept pace with the emerging positive trend line was a key to his success. Things were harder now since the company had been sold by a multinational corporation to a private equity firm interested in only one thing: flipping the business for a substantial profit in three to five years. To the new owners, people were numbers in what was only a numbers game. Dan knew it, and he had been looking for other work since the takeover. But timing is everything, and everything about the timing sucked.

Due to the number of miles he flew each year Dan was in first class, so he boarded early to get a drink. He ordered a scotch on the rocks, took the small cup of nuts and ate them like taking a shot, and sat back to stare out at the activity on the tarmac below.

His mind started to wander to Las Vegas and to poker. He was a novice. He had picked up an interest for the game when a few of his golfing buddies started to watch the World Series of poker on television.

Dan was learning. He played online for play money when he was on the road and alone in some Holiday Inn Express. He had played live with his buddies a few times, but never in a casino. He brought a book with him to read on the plane that had chapters on the best hands, the worst hands, strategies for figuring out "tells", strategies for playing and betting positions, and even poker etiquette.

He put the book down when dinner came. The flight attendant filled his wine glass and he ate the ravioli with a side salad and bread. He ignored the cookie. He finished off the wine, put his napkin in the glass to prevent another re-fill, hit the button on the armrest to recline his seat, kicked off his shoes, and closed his eyes.

He felt a hand on his shoulder. It was the flight attendant gently waking him up for landing. A weaker than usual head wind allowed the flight to land about twenty minutes ahead of schedule. He brought his seat back to the upright position and took off the earphones. He put his book into his briefcase and put the case back in the overhead for landing. He sat back down, buckled up, and looked down at the neon below.

It was 8:55 p.m. Las Vegas time when Dan passed the electronic key over the sensor to room 34 144. Dan quickly put the suitcase down in the corner of the room, placed his briefcase under the small desk in the work area, and checked his pockets for cash and his key. He left the room at exactly 9:02 p.m. He forgot to call his wife, which he was always supposed to do when he arrived somewhere. This time it would not matter until the morning, since she was fast asleep, it being a few minutes after midnight in Northern Kentucky.

Chapter 3

Anyone who has looked up at the ceiling in a casino has seen the infamous "eye in the sky." Little black domes hide cameras that watch every table, every dealer, every player, every cocktail waitress, everybody. The technicians who monitor the myriad screens taking the video feed from the "eye in the sky" are highly trained professionals adept at spotting potential cheats, liars, thieves, and deviates. Because first rate security means belt, suspenders, and a backup for those, the "eye in the sky" is supplemented with cat walks above the ceiling where trained private security walk over the gaming tables and peer down through one way glass.

It is disconcerting. There could be someone watching your hands, your legs, looking down your wife's blouse, taking video of your lip movements and reading them, all while you ignorantly feed the beast with your cash.

On this day, security was taking an interest in a man playing at table fifteen, seat eight in the poker room. He had been erratic, his hands were often not visible, and by way of lip reading his comments and mood were inconsistent. More importantly, he had turned a corner and was now winning pretty regularly.

Casinos don't mind losing to a point, which is what brings everyone back. But casinos loathe losing to "cheaters." The "eye in the sky" was suspicious that perhaps the Brit was one of these. They would keep a close watch to find out one way or the other.

From time to time, the Brit would put one hand or both hands into the pockets of his heavily worn herring bone red sport coat. His hands seemed to fidget in his pockets. And the Brit was always dropping something, which would give him an excuse to drop his entire upper body out of sight of the table for a second or two. What was he doing down there?

He also had arrived at the table with two bright yellow hundred dollar chips from a casino in London, which he fiddled with nervously at almost all times. These chips drew comments from other players more than once, indicating that they were attention getters.

The Brit would always say the same thing, "Don't worry mates, these chips aren't in play, they're just good luck pieces for me. It's nothing to excite you about, is it now?"

Diversion is the oldest trick in the magician's book, the security guys were thinking. And they kept watching.

As the cameras panned over him and the catwalk above him was occupied more often than not, the Brit played the game that put bread on the table for him and his wife. The tics continued, the mannerisms remained unpredictable, and his stack grew larger. It was just past 9:00 p.m. and he had recovered his $800 buy in, long forgotten about the three Queens beaten by the three Aces, and had almost $1,800 in chips. He was right on target for his $1,000 a day, but time was now his enemy. He was an addict. He could not stop playing even when pre-established goals were made. Quite simply, it was too early to quit.

On the next hand, the Brit got a two and a seven, considered the worst hand in Texas hold'em. He folded it. That wouldn't give the guys in the sky anything to go on. The one thing they could not see was the cards face down and mucked.

His next hand was much better, and as he was looking at it under cupped hands, the player in seat nine declared himself out and went to get a plastic rack to carry his chips to the cashier. As he looked at his King, Queen suited, he also considered that he would soon have a new player immediately to his left.

On this relatively strong hand he was in late position, which made it even better. No one in front of him raised the bet, and half of them folded. He used one of his favorite strategies, to toss $13 in chips onto the table, twirling them on their way to the felt, and effectively raising $10 to the others.

Three players called him, and the flop brought two cards in his suit, giving him a high flush draw possibility. When the action got to him after all checked bets, he raised another $13. Only one other player called, leaving it heads up.

The turn made his flush, King high. Now he was smoking. The other player bet $10, which the Brit viewed as a pussy bet. He knew his foe was weak. If I go too high, he thought, this guy's out. I'll suck a few more dollars out by raising $20; he'll stick around to see the river for that. The guy bit, the river did not help him, and the pot was raked in and added to the Brit's growing stack.

The cameras in the ceiling kept rolling.

Chapter 4

Despite contrary appearances at the table in Las Vegas, the Brit had a pedigree. His father was a high ranking officer in the Royal Navy, and his mother was a daughter of the same. The family was well known, well liked, and extremely well respected in London, in all of England for that matter. He was an only son, who grew up with an often absent father. His mother and grandmother raised him for the most part, and he always had been independent. He fancied himself a free thinker, an individual more concerned with living than with the influences of the world around him.

His early years were unremarkable. He was well-adjusted and made his milestones for childhood development at or in front of the expected pace. He seemed to those around him to be a happy tot. He was reasonably sociable. He had good manners. He made his way through his first school years without incident and in fine academic form.

Unlike most of the young people around him he always took responsibility for his actions, good, bad, or indifferent.

After primary school he went to the Rochester Independent College in Kent County, just east of

London. He was a boarder there from sixteen until university, even though he lived within an easy commute. The school was perfect for him. It was a progressive school, where no uniforms were worn, no bells were rung (as is the case with most prestigious English prep schools), and everyone was on a first name basis including the instructors. Perhaps most importantly for the Brit freedom of thought was not only encouraged but implicitly demanded. There were no academic or curricular boundaries. He felt free to choose how to respond to the painful existence of school.

He became an adult at Rochester, learning to live on his own socially and emotionally if not economically. He made friends and had a close knit band of mates among the 60 or so boarders. He was popular with the girls, charming and ebullient. He was not overly athletic, but participated in football and cricket as was expected of everyone at the school. He was a good teammate.

He did not look forward to university, but he reluctantly understood that the next step was inevitable and he dutifully resigned himself to it.

His father managed to get away from his military duties to attend his graduation from Rochester with his mother.

At luncheon after the commencement exercises, his father lectured and deposed him:

"So, lad, your time here is finished and I trust it was well spent. Now bigger challenges await you. Your mother and I have talked about it quite extensively, and we feel Oxford is the better choice over Cambridge. We are confident you agree. The question is what will you make of yourself?"

"I rather fancy writing father, and I'd hoped to take a year or two off from formal studies to pursue that. I'd rather live than learn just for the sake of knowing things."

The look on his father's face was enough to clearly convey his displeasure with the notion. His father put his fork down on the plate slowly and deliberately. He finished chewing and wiped his mouth with the linen napkin. He placed the napkin correctly on his lap. Before he spoke he took a small sip of the white wine.

"That's really out of the question, my boy. It's quite simply out of the question. Pure rubbish, it is. And to think you have that notion after all you have been provided to this point. I've always said every endeavor must be finished, every job completed to the best of one's ability. You know that, boy. I have always made that quite clear. Mother?"

His mother was obliged to answer with the party line, although the strain in her voice belied her conviction, "Father is right, son. There's too much invested at this point, and the family name is placed at issue. There will be time enough to follow your writing ambition, but after a proper and complete education. It is important to know things in order to live properly. How can you suggest that it is not?" She paused for an emphasis, smiled at him, and continued. "You must finish what we have all started. Come now, you've always known that."

She smiled at him again, this time like he was a little child. He did not smile back.

There was silence as the three munched slowly on the salad of field greens with bits of fish. No one looked up from their platters for a short while.

His father broke the tension, "I was a young bloke once too, you know. Hard to imagine it I reckon, but true enough it is. I had similar talks with my father and he prevailed," and he sipped his wine, and then said confidently, "as will we."

He put his glass down and placed his elbow on the table.

"And in retrospect, how glad I am that he did. You will be too, trust me."

The Brit replied, "How can you be so sure, father? One can't know what one hasn't known, right? What did you aspire to do, and why did grandfather talk you out of it?"

"It's of no matter, son. The point is that triviality and dalliance are in the minds of the young as a matter of nature's course, and we adults are mindful of our obligation to right that course. I have navigated all of my adult life, and I intend to navigate now. I will, mind you, keep you in charted waters."

Again there was an awkward silence broken only by the sound of silverware striking lightly against the fine china.

His mother tried to change the topic, "What a nice ceremony, don't you think?"

No one answered.

The Brit placed his silverware in the middle of his plate and pushed it ever so slightly away from him to indicate he was finished with his lunch. He mustered up more resolve and he plowed on, "I'm very much counting on some time to explore writing. What harm would a few years sabbatical from school do? I think you make too much of the things that are taught in school. Rather superficial, it seems to me. Even then, there is time enough to finish school if the writing experiment doesn't work out."

His father stiffened and straightened in his chair and his voice grew stern, "Enough. You're talking immature nonsense, and I'll have no more. This is not a negotiation. This is a family decision, and it has been made."

The Brit's father sat back and winced. He turned to his wife.

"Let's finish lunch and take a walk by the river. Wouldn't that be nice mother?"

"Yes, quite," she said, averting her gaze toward a down trodden and wholly defeated young graduate.

As they walked on the river bank, the Brit stayed several paces behind his parents, throwing sticks and stones into the river and watching them disappear beneath the surface. They walked on without speaking. There did not seem to be anything left to say.

The Brit matriculated at the University of Oxford the following fall, choosing the Humanities Department and embarking on the course in Studies of Voltaire and the 18th Century. Generally, he was unenthused. Occasionally he was engaged. For example, he was fascinated by the poem that explored the randomness of the Lisbon earthquake of 1755. He kept a copy beneath his pillow.

At the end, and as he would have readily summarized, his time at Oxford was not particularly noteworthy. He managed to graduate, without distinction. His father had grown distant as the Brit continuously failed to meet his expectations. His mother played the role of mediator between the two, as best as she could.

After graduation from Oxford, the Brit took a position teaching Voltaire in a public secondary school. His heart was not in it. He started to write at night. His heart was not in that either. A few of the other instructors played poker each Wednesday night after a quick supper at a local pub. He started to join them, and his heart was in it.

He turned to the study of poker more fervently than he had committed to any study before. He learned quickly. Within a few months the Brit had outgrown the little friendly game on Wednesday nights. He started to visit the casinos in London and had some modest success. He surmised he could make more playing poker than he was making as a teacher, and he asked to go on part-time status. Soon, he up and quit teaching, and was in the casinos every day and most of every night.

On one night in early March, he returned after a light supper to the table at his favorite poker room. As he waited for a seat, he noticed a very attractive lady playing at a table with higher stakes than he typically played. He could not take his eyes off of her, and when he was presented with a seat at his regular game, he declined and joined the wait list for her table. He kept his eyes on her and on her stack of chips to make sure she was not close to leaving. Finally, he was called to the table. He had hoped for a seat near to her, but his seat was opposite from her and a long way away. He waited and waited for a seat beside her to open up and once it did he immediately requested a seat change, which request was granted by the dealer.

"Hello," he said to her as he sat down and piled his chips in order before him. He pulled out his two yellow chips and started juggling them back and forth from hand to hand.

She nodded back.

"Just trying to be friendly," he said. "Nothing wrong with being friendly, is there?"

She ignored him.

He turned to the player on his left and said, "Pretty intense, isn't she? I'm just trying to be friendly. Nothing wrong with trying to be friendly is what I always say, right mate?"

He ignored him too.

Although there may be friendly poker games going on all over the world at any given time, there are rarely friendly games at the casino. Up until tonight that had suited the Brit just fine, but it wasn't working for him now.

"This has been a hot seat," he tried again. "I've been watching. Noticed you too, you know. Sure did. Paid right close attention to you I did."

"Look, sir," she said, "I chat at other places, but not here, ok?"

"Ah, a chink in the old armor," he said. "A sliver of daylight I see I do."

"That is a blatant misinterpretation of the situation, sir."

"Ah, I don't know. I see you coming 'round little by little."

"Just play, sir. That's all I want to do. Just play."

He stiffened and pretended to agree.

"Right. Know the feeling."

He fell silent and looked to be in deep thought.

"Alright. I understand your position completely, been there myself. So here's the deal, no pun intended," and he smiled. "I promise to shut up if you will have lunch with me at one of the places where you do chat and socialize."

He waited for a long time before she answered.

"If you really keep your mouth shut for the rest of the time I am here, and I mean not even a sigh, I'll agree for the sake of my sanity tonight."

With a gesture he zipped his mouth shut with his hand. And he stayed true to his word, as painful as it was for him. When the game was winding down, he took a cocktail napkin and scribbled "1:00 Friday, The Lion's Head on Shrewsbury."

She picked up the napkin and stuffed it into her purse.

He did not play poker on Friday morning. He paced in his small flat. He watched the clock and paced some more.

At 12:30 he locked the door behind him, and went to the curb to start his old, heavily worn Volvo. He arrived at the Lion's Head at ten minutes before one.

"A booth for two, please, I'm waiting on someone."

The pert young hostess led him to a booth and took his drink order.

"Beefeater's and tonic, lime," he said, and settled in and waited.

At 1:15 he ordered another, and looked at the clock on the wall.

She's standing me up, he thought. He sipped his drink. What did you expect, he asked himself.

He was taking the second sip of his second drink when he heard her.

"Sorry to be late, but I was outside reconsidering."

"No need to be sorry," he said. "Please, sit down," and he stood clumsily as she was seated.

"What were you reconsidering?"

"What do you think?"

"Oh, right. Rather obvious, isn't it?"

"It is."

"What can I order you to drink?"

"I can order for myself."

"Oh, alright then. Sure."

He was reconsidering now. Women are difficult, he thought. Why did everything have to be so hard?

The waiter approached and she ordered, "A Bloody Mary, extra spicy."

Things got better. They talked about all sorts of things over lunch. She was from a working class family in Leeds and had moved to London to get work as a waitress at the casino. She started to play blackjack first on her off days, and then tried her hand at poker. She had become almost as obsessed with it as he had. And she was having success, which explained her seat at the higher stakes table.

She was not impressed by his background, which he found refreshing. She was impressed with his openness and honesty. They talked for a long time about a lot of things.

They were married within three months.

Chapter 5

It was 9:35 when Dan Berry from Bromley Kentucky was finally offered a seat in the poker room. He had waited for about twenty five minutes since he had been on the casino floor. He was getting a bit tired after the long day, the long flight, and on account of the time difference. It was 12:35 Wednesday morning back home.

He sat down at seat nine, next to a man with a motley red sport coat, now wearing a white Fedora.

Dan looked around the table, moving clockwise. At seat ten there was an obese man with a University of Arkansas tee shirt that stretched out and struggled to cover his enormous belly. The man was unshaven, probably for at least three days, and was sipping coffee from a large paper cup. Next was the dealer, a diminutive Asian woman, who was trying to lighten the mood with a smile. She's cute, Dan thought. At seat one there was a tall, thin man in a shirt and tie, with the tie loosened and the shirt wrinkled. He was grimacing and squinting; he seemed to be in pain. The cards were being dealt and Dan continued to survey the field. At seat two a woman with tattooed arms and a Santana bandana was playing with her chips and chewing gum nervously. Dan looked down at his cards and mucked a six, nine. At seat three a grey haired man with sunglasses and a white soul patch stared off somewhere into the distance. Player five raked in a small pot. At seat four there was a reserved button in front of an empty seat; someone was taking a break. At seat five a middle aged black man sat behind a large stack of chips. He had a toothpick in his mouth and he switched it from side to side with precision and ease. At seat six a tall, pretty blonde woman in a tight black dress bent over to show off her cleavage. She was the only one with a cocktail. At seat seven an Asian man with tobacco stained teeth sat motionless. His breathing was shallow and labored. Was he awake? And then there was seat eight. The Brit was on a high, with large stacks of chips including one stack of $100 chips. Dan noticed without much effort that the Brit was the chip leader at the table. Just a few minutes before Dan's arrival, the Brit had taken a bathroom break. He was non-stop chatter.

"Keep the cards coming, sweetheart," he said, flipping the yellow chips from one hand to the other.

He grew stern and said, "Sir, you're calling out of turn. Seriously, sir, that's not right. It'll influence what the players in front of you will do. Please, sir, stay in turn."

The dealer rolled her eyes. No one paid any attention to the Brit. They had all been there too long.

Dan found him entertaining. He took the bait. "Doing pretty well, I see," he said to the Brit.

"A friendly bloke, by God," blurted out the Brit, and he put his hand on Dan's shoulder. "It's about fricking time. I thought I was playing at Madame Tussaud's wax museum. They actually have one here in Vegas, you know, and for about the last hour I've been thinking I made a wrong turn and sat down at a table there, with these mannequins," and he gestured around the table with a clockwise wave of his arm.

Dan laughed.

"Where're you from, mate?"

"Bromley, Kentucky."

"Bromley, Kentucky. Really? Is it near Louisville? Bluegrass and all that?"

"Closer to Cincinnati, but the bluegrass part you got."

"Ah, yes. Land of the thoroughbred, mate, I know it well from the tellie. Partial to the ponies, are you?"

"I go once in a while, to Turfway that is."

"Wouldn't be good for me, to be that close I mean. I wouldn't get any sleep at all if there was decent racing to be bet on. Except for a strong hand here, there's nothing like the sound of the thundering herd coming 'round the final turn heading for home. Like I say, nothing except maybe for this, eh? Better than sex, mate, better than sex I'll wager."

"Right," Dan said, and he realized that he was next to a lunatic or an addict or both.

The Brit looked at his cards. He had an Ace, ten non-suited. Dan looked at his cards. He had Kings. He looked at his cards again and then looked around the table to see if anyone noticed that he had looked at his cards twice. Dan wondered if the poker face he was trying so hard to put on was working at all. He didn't know where or how to look. He thought it was funny how self-conscious he felt just because he finally got a couple of good cards. "Drinks," the cocktail waitress said looking at Dan, and he nervously waved her away. The Brit saw it all, and smiled to himself without moving his mouth or lips on the outside.

After a round of low ball betting, the dealer placed the burn card face down and flopped three cards, a

King, a Jack, and a six. Dan twitched when he saw his third King and his right leg started bobbing up and down with nervous energy. The Brit quietly and imperceptibly shuddered inside, knowing he had only a gut shot straight draw as a likely winner and knowing that Dan was ready to jump out of his skin because of the high hand he was holding.

Any bet by Dan would have pushed the Brit out. But Dan was stymied. He lacked experience. He made the mistake of trying the "slow play" at a time when only an amateur would try it. The pot was big enough, and he should have bet high to drive the Brit to fold and to take the chips then for himself.

"Check," Dan said.

"Check," the Brit said, happy to get a look at his only out card for free.

The dealer put out the turn card. It was a four.

Dan misplayed again. He bet only $20, hoping to get a few more out of the Brit.

But this was not enough to keep the Brit out of the possibility of a big pot.

"Call," said the Brit.

The dealer showed the river card.

It was a Queen.

Dan, the amateur, was overjoyed it was not an Ace and wrongly calculated that he was a sure winner. He never considered the possibility of a straight. He failed to stop to consider and think.

"All in," he said, and he pushed all his chips into the middle of the table.

The Brit could not believe his ears. Quickly assessing, he determined that it was not possible for him to lose. There was no four of a kind possibility, there was no full house possibility, there was no flush possibility, and there was no higher straight possibility.

"I call," he said, with a big smile and a flamboyant flip of the cards to show the Ace high straight.

Dan was crushed. He showed his Kings to save face among the other players and congratulated the Brit, who was paying no attention to his new friend now. While the Brit celebrated Dan got up quietly to go up to bed. It had only been forty-five minutes for Dan and already $250 was gone.

The Brit was busily arranging his stack in a new order; it was growing higher by the hour. He never noticed Dan leaving the table.

It was only 10:30 p.m. The Brit looked at his stack and then looked at his watch. Uncharacteristically, and with sensibility and sanity not often expressed, the Brit announced he was out. He went to the cashier's window to retrieve trays on which to place all of his chips. He came back to the table with five trays, and realized that would not be enough. He got three more and filled seven and some. Each tray could hold $500 in chips. A quick count showed he had about $3800. He nearly had reached his objective in only one day. At this rate, he thought to himself, I will knock this session out of the park, borrowing an American sports analogy for good luck and good measure.

The Brit took his booty to the cashier, who counted out thirty seven one hundred dollar bills and four twenty dollar bills; the Brit had exactly $3,780, $9,000 still in his room, and three and a half days left to play.

The Brit had not accounted for an early quit and he had taken chemicals throughout the day to ensure an all-nighter. Now, he had to compensate for this chemical imbalance. With a large wad of cash, and a fair deal of swagger, he entered the bar at the Prime Steakhouse, an upscale restaurant on the promenade level of the casino. Despite the hour it was still crowded with diners, but the bar was empty.

The Brit sat down and ordered a Tanqueray martini up with blue cheese stuffed olives. He fiddled with two yellow chips on the bar counter. When the bartender set his cocktail in front of him, he lifted it and drained half in one large swig. The bartender noted it as odd.

The Brit finished his first drink quickly and ordered a second. He realized that sleep would have to be induced against a powerful amphetamine counter weight. While he waited for the bartender to mix his drink, he stared at his cell phone and realized he had not phoned his wife since his arrival. He knew that she would not find this alarming or unusual given their lifestyles and the time difference, but he lamented the gap that seemed to have grown between them. At first, they would play in the same room at the Golden Nugget. But now, with ever increasing frequency, he played at the Napoleons and she played at The Palm Beach. They crossed paths during cat naps between sessions, and he was struggling to remember the last time that they had sex. Money was a constant strain. When they had it they knew it was at great risk. When they didn't have it, it was even worse.

He tried to imagine her. Could he remember exactly how her hair was fixed? He could not. Did he know whether she had gained weight or lost weight recently? He guessed that she had lost, but he was not sure. Was she was shaving her legs each day? There was no way for him to know that. Who was this woman who he lived with? Oddly enough, he missed her for a second.

The Brit flipped the phone closed and took a sip, not a gulp, this time. He decided sedation would be a slow, deliberate process, which could not be rushed against the biological forces working against it.

Chapter 6

It was a little before 11:00 p.m. when the Brit noticed an attractive middle aged lady sit down at the other side of the circular bar at the Prime. She was dressed in a conservative, grey business suit, but her blouse was open several buttons, just enough to interest the Brit. She had black glasses, but they looked right and good on her. He could only see her from the waist up, but he liked what he saw. She had dark hair, delicate features, and an alarming smile. He watched as she ordered a Cosmopolitan. He could not hear the conversation, but it seemed like she knew the bartender.

The Brit was fortified with speed and liquor. He picked up his drink and sauntered around the bar and sat one seat away from her, not overplaying his hand. She stiffened, knowing the drill and not particularly liking it. The bartender sent her a glance as if to say do you want me to cut this off? She signaled back that she could handle it, for now at least.

"Hi, there, lovely," the Brit said, spinning his bar stool around so he faced her directly.

"Hello," she said, without much looking at him.

"I hope I'm not being too forward, but I'm just looking for a little friendly conversation before retiring. Really, no ulterior motives here, ma'am, none whatsoever, I promise you."

His accent was charming, and she let her guard down a bit. She turned a quarter turn to look at him. He was unkempt, but not unattractive. His eyes were dilated like saucers, so she knew he was on some sort of crank, and she knew this was not good. She decided to put it out there to diffuse any further problems.

"Look, I have no reason to not believe you about the ulterior motives, but I have lived in Vegas for fifteen years and I have no earthly reason to believe you either. So let's just understand each other," and she took a drink before continuing, "just in case you're another liar passing through sin city. I'm a lesbian. And no, you're not the man who is going to turn me around. And, yes, it's true, not just a ruse to throw you off of the scent."

"That's fascinating honesty. Bravo for that," the Brit replied. "It's so good to hear someone speak freely and clearly. It might have taken me weeks or months to find that out from many people. Why is that?"

"I don't know. I guess some people are uncomfortable with their own realities." She paused a moment to reflect. "Sometimes not knowing someone keeps things alive and delays the inevitable. You know what I mean?"

"Absolutely, love. Absolutely, I do. Fascinating, brilliant it all is."

He was starting to slur his words. He took a long drink.

"What brings you here? Are you staying in the hotel?"

"No, I live here."

"Really, fancy that. Do you work in the casino?"

"No, no. I'm a lawyer with a practice downtown. I just finished speaking at a conference in one of the meeting rooms."

"Really? A barrister, eh? Well I might need one of those someday, right? Just might indeed. Do you have a card?"

She hesitated. Oh, what the hell, she thought. The card did not have any personal contact information and there were always dozens of people around the office. She pulled out a card and handed it to the Brit.

He looked at the card slowly and carefully. Mary F. Roys, Attorney at Law, Dunham and Dunham PLLC, 3918 Rainbow Boulevard, Las Vegas NV…

"So, Mary, what kind of law do you practice?"

"I'm a litigator. Mostly I defend corporations and manufacturers in toxic tort lawsuits. Pretty much all defense work."

"Toxic torts?" he said, with a queer look on his face.

She smiled, sensing his confusion.

"Yeah, cases where people say they got sick from exposure to chemicals or some other toxic substance. Not a very flattering name, is it?" She paused and said quickly, "Not much of anything flattering about it, come to think of it."

"I'm not so sure, love. Interesting to me it is."

"Hard to believe," she said, and she sipped her drink.

He seemed to her now to be innocent enough, and to understand that a one night hook-up was out of the question. She grew more at ease now that she felt it was just conversation.

"What were you speaking about tonight, to the other lawyers at your meeting I mean?"

"I guarantee you don't want to know," she said, with a light laugh.

"Indeed, I do," he said, insistently.

"I'm really sure you don't," she said, with a confidence that only piqued his curiosity.

"I insist that you tell me or I shall start a hunger strike immediately," and he leapt down from the bar stool and did a Ghandi impersonation, sitting cross-legged on the barroom floor. She was laughing loudly now.

When she stopped laughing she said, "Seriously, do you really want to know, because it's not cocktail conversation?"

"I have nothing but time until this gin brings me to a place where I can sleep. And I have days before I'll require a tube for feeding."

She knew he had won.

"OK, if you really insist. I gave a talk on the latest medical and epidemiological literature on whether exposure to a chemical called benzene causes acute promyelocytic leukemia."

His mouth was open. "What? And I could've starved for that?"

"I told you it wasn't what you wanted to talk about."

"You were right."

They both laughed. The Brit got up and perched himself back on the bar stool. She spoke again.

"So now you know why I'm here, what about you?"

"Now I must reverse the situation. Are you sure you're interested?"

"No, but it's only fair since you asked me."

"Honest to a fault, I dare say. A peach, isn't she?"

"So, hurry up. I have to work in the morning," she said, and took another small sip.

"My wife sent me here to change my luck at the gaming tables. I'm from London, in case you couldn't tell from the accent, Bloomsbury to be exact. Maybe you've heard of our football club?" He paused for a response and there wasn't one. "She, my wife that is, isn't right about much, but so far she seems to have gotten this one spot on."

He felt bad that he had said his wife wasn't right about much. The feeling passed.

He went on, "Funny, really. But I think you'd like my wife. She spent quite a bit of time at the University of Leeds advocating for gay and lesbian rights at a time when it was right unpopular to do so?"

"Really," she said, "what got her into that?"

"She had a friend from her childhood in Leeds who was teased and harassed mercilessly when the others found out she fancied girls, sometime around secondary school I guess, and my wife apparently couldn't stomach the foul treatment. She really took it on as a cause. Did some good, if I say so myself."

"That's cool," Mary said.

She glanced at her watch and took a bit of her drink.

"So you are winning?"

"So far, yes. And I have three and a half days left to play. Time is interesting. In this case, it may be my downfall. I almost wish I was at the airport, far from the tables, with cash in my pocket. But here, with time and money, I can't resist the impulse to play on. It's insane."

"Not to get too personal, but could you stop gambling if you tried?"

"I wouldn't even try. The question is moot, as you barristers would say."

She glanced at her watch. It was nearly midnight.

"I have to go," she said.

"Pity," he said. "True pity, it is."

"Did you really find this conversation that pleasant?"

"No, bugger that" he said. "Pity you like girls, isn't it?" and he looked her up and down from head to toe. He stood and tipped his hat to her.

They shook hands politely and she walked away. She nodded good-bye to the bartender. The Brit watched her leave the bar and his eyes followed her all the way down the long corridor until she turned right, toward the escalator near the entrance to the casino spa. He was looking at her ass when she disappeared around the corner.

What a waste of a pretty woman, he thought. But not for the other woman who has her, he corrected himself.

He was now finishing his third martini. His eyelids were getting heavy. The excitement of the poker session, the three big drinks, and the jet lag finally setting in all combined to beat back the amphetamines. He thought he was ready to try to sleep.

He paid cash for his tab. But unlike most gamblers with recent winnings, he did not leave an extraordinary tip, rather one on the meager side.

The Brit walked out onto the promenade deck and started for the elevator when he stopped abruptly and leaned against the railing. Should he call his wife? Why not, he thought?

He calculated what time it would be in London, and then he realized that the time of day was not relevant to a decision on when to call a compulsive gambler.

He took out his cell phone and dialed the number.

After several rings, she picked up.

"Hello, love. How's it going," he opened.

"Call you back in a few," and she hung up abruptly.

He heard the casino noises in the background, so he knew she was playing.

He waited for a few minutes. He looked down at his phone to make sure the ringer was on. He went into the gift shop and bought a bag of salt and vinegar chips. He finished the chips. He looked at his watch. He knew she was not going to call back.

He headed for the elevators. When he got to his room he carefully took the cash out of his pocket and counted it again to make sure none had disappeared since leaving the table. He opened the safe in the room and counted out the $9,000 that he had left to make sure it was all still there. Then he carefully replaced the money, in one pile with exactly $10,000 and in another pile with the balance, the winnings pile.

He brushed his teeth and undressed slowly. He left his skivvies on. He put Mary Roy's card into his wallet next to his credit cards. He closed his eyes and imagined her ass one more time. He dropped straight back onto the bed and, amazingly, he was asleep within minutes.

With the combination of drugs and alcohol, he had forgotten to lock and latch the door.

Chapter 7

The following morning at 9:00 a.m. Mary Roys entered the meeting room at the Convention Center Marriott to set up for the deposition of an industrial hygienist in one of her cases pending in Madison County IL. The plaintiff's lawyer, from St. Louis, had agreed to Las Vegas as the location for the deposition for the obvious reason of wanting to mix some pleasure with the trip. And the expert witness, from Los Angeles, was an avid poker player, so he was more than willing to spend the day being questioned by Ms. Roys, in exchange for a night in the casino.

Mary had deposed this guy many times before and she knew he would not give a straight answer to any of her questions. She had resigned herself several depositions ago to be satisfied with making a record of his failures and refusals to answer. She knew the drill, he knew the drill, and they started the drill promptly at 9:30 a.m., when the witness was sworn to tell the truth by the court reporter.

As Mary started her questioning, the Brit was slowly waking up across town. He slept longer than he anticipated, and when he saw the clock he had a brief but strong panic attack. When he went to the bathroom he glanced toward the hotel room door, which was slightly ajar. He could see through the crack into the hallway outside. His heart jumped into his throat.

"Shit," he said very out loud. The Brit sprinted to the door and shut it. He scampered to the safe with his zipper open and his belt undone. He noted that the safe was locked, but this did not comfort him at all. His hands shook violently as he struggled to punch in the combination to the safe. It took him three tries.

When the safe door was opened, he stuck his hands in violently in search of cash. He breathed a temporary sigh of relief when his right hand felt a stack of bills, and he was almost entirely calmed when his left hand found another smaller stack.

He pulled both piles of money out of the safe and began to count furiously. He tripled checked both stacks, and it was all there.

What happened, he thought to himself. Did I leave it open? Was someone in here? Is something else missing?

He went to the nightstand next to his bed and snatched up his wallet. He looked through all of his drawers, and he looked into the desk cubbies.

Everything seemed ok. But his paranoia ran rampant and he could not think straight.

Where was his cell phone? He found it right where he thought he left it.

"Shit, this is making me crazy," he said aloud again. "How flipping stoned was I?" He rubbed his temples and craned his neck back to stretch out the tension. "I hate this bloody feeling."

The Brit locked and latched the door after checking every nook and cranny of the room to make sure no intruder was in hiding. He pushed the privacy button near the door, and headed for the shower. But his mind continued to race as water cascaded over him, and a headache was slowly starting to build across the bridge of his forehead.

He tried to let the hot water pull out the pain and massage his sore head. It worked some, and he stood there motionless for several minutes as he cleansed his mind.

Mary Roys was on the first break at the deposition when the Brit finished dressing and made ready to head to the poker room.

Dan had been at the first day of the trade show since about 8:30. It was his responsibility to open the booth every morning now, since David had begged off of the trip at the last minute because his son was sick. Opening at 8:30 in Vegas was a joke, and everyone knew it. No one would arrive before 10:00, and most would not be coherent until after eating lunch. But David was counting on him to open, and so he did.

By mid-morning, traffic at the booth had picked up, and Dan was hitting his stride with his sales pitch.

"Acrylic is a superior product for signage because of its UV properties. Sure, it costs more, but it will still look great after baking in the Florida sun for years. That other stuff will be faded, and will reflect poorly on your business and on your pocketbook when it has to be replaced. This is the wise choice; can I get your card for our files?"

He had similar spiels for bath tubs, hot tubs, and kitchen countertops. He could recite each in his sleep. It was a mindless repetition, and he said it so often he truly believed it.

At his lunch break, he walked across the street to the lobby café in the Marriott. He took lunch by himself at the counter, and he could not help but notice an attractive middle aged professional poring over a legal pad and frantically scribbling notes with one hand and shoveling salad into her face with the other. She never looked up until her salad was gone. When she did, their eyes met, and he nodded to her. She smiled and nodded back. Mary Roys picked up her papers and put them into her briefcase. She wiped her mouth with the napkin, touched up her lipstick, and primped her hair. She got up and threw down a twenty dollar bill, picked up her case, and headed back to the meeting room for the rest of the deposition.

Dan finished his turkey club sandwich and ate half of his pickle. He took a final swig of his water and paid the tab. He snatched up the receipt and shoved it into his shirt pocket. Dan belched and got up to return to the booth. He would have to stay until 5:30. There was a cocktail reception to follow the official close of the show for the first day, but since David was not here he would skip it. He had not been able to get his last poker hand out of his head and he had already decided to play more, even though he had now crossed the threshold of what he could afford to lose for entertainment. He needed to win now and he meant to do just that.

Everyone always looked forward to the sweepstakes drawing at the show which took place at 3:00 in the afternoon on the first day. It worked like this: every employee at a booth of an exhibitor was automatically entered in the cash sweepstakes. At 2:55, a giant carnival wheel, with numbers from one to eighteen, would spin round and round until it stopped on a number. That number would be multiplied by $1,000 and the product of the multiplication would be the cash prize amount for the drawing to follow.

Last year, Dan was remembering, a cute sales lady from his biggest competitor won $9,000. And the prize was handed out in cold, hard cash. Maybe this year would be his year.

Dan was getting tired and bored around 2:30, so he got a cup of coffee and tried to pick up his spirits for the drawing, which would at least signal the halfway point to the afternoon being over. At the coffee station, he saw his old friend Bill Bronson.

"Hey Bill," Dan called over.

"Dan, my man," Bill fired back.

The two walked toward each other, coffees in hand.

"How're things, Dan?"

"About the same, Bill," he said. "What about with you?"

"Well, got a divorce six months ago. That's been a game changer. The kids are just getting around to accepting it, and I don't think Becky ever will. She read my texts and found out about my road antics. I always knew it was risky, but like they said when I hit the road, it's hazardous duty."

"That sucks, man. Sorry to hear it. Do the kids know why you split up?"

"Yeah, and it's not helped my status with them. Even when they're acting normally, my paranoia kicks in and I feel like they're stabbing me with their eyes."

"I bet, man. Wow."

"So much for that, what's up with you?"

"We've been trying to get pregnant."

There was an uncomfortable pause.

Dan kept on, "I have mixed feelings, but she doesn't. So far nothing's happened, but I'm on a sex schedule now so at least it's good for planning."

Bill laughed, relieved that this would not be a serious conversation.

"No shit, she tells me to hump her like she's telling me to take out the trash. It's weird."

Their conversation was interrupted by the announcement, "The sweepstakes wheel spins in one minute. One minute to pegging this year's prize."

"How many people are in this damn thing?" Bill asked.

"I think about forty," Dan wondered more than answered.

"Not bad odds. I could use the cash."

"Tell me about it."

They both moved closer to the crowd gathering around the wheel near the center of the exhibition floor. The marketing VP from the year's primary show sponsor took the honors for spinning the wheel. Dan thought he looked like a real geek, and when the VP opened his mouth Dan's opinion was confirmed.

After a short introduction welcoming everyone to the show, he finally pulled on the wheel and let it rip.

The wheel landed on thirteen. In a few minutes, one of the forty or so would win $13,000.

Dan went back to his booth where activity was moderate. He chatted briefly with a buyer from South Korea, who was there no doubt to gather intelligence and had no intention of buying anything. Dan knew and adjusted his pitch appropriately. A little disinformation is sometimes better than real information or no information, and Dan took full advantage with his minute or so of opportunity. Bastard, he thought.

The Korean man walked away and the drawing was at hand.

A paid part-time model, probably full-time stripper or hooker, who was among the other paid part-time "models" hired to walk around the floor as eye candy, moved to the large transparent bin. She was holding forty or so slips of paper with forty or so names on them.

The "model" turned the crank to spin the bin, and the men egged her on to keep cranking because her large silicone breasts heaved mechanically with each bend and turn. She bent forward ever so slightly to improve the view. Once the spinning and jiggling was over, she bent over at the waist and reached into the small window. She pulled out a slip of paper and handed it to the geek.

In a shrill voice he said, "And the winner is …. Dan Berry."

Dan yelled out loudly, "Holy shit, that's me."

All of his colleagues applauded and those in closest proximity congratulated him, all of which was disingenuous. They were all pissed.

After all of the back slapping, Dan was escorted to the show office, and he watched as the woman at the desk filled a small silver case with one hundred and thirty $100 bills.

Sorry, David, he thought. He left early, clutching the case under his arm like he was protecting a football near the goal line. He walked briskly toward the cab stand in front of the Convention Center and got a cab back to the hotel. He never hesitated, stopped, or diverted his gaze as he walked with purpose to the elevators.

When he walked into his room he immediately locked the door and pressed the privacy button. He placed the case on the small table in front of the sitting chair and unlatched it. He opened the case and pulled out one stack of the ten stacks of thirteen

$100 bills. He fanned it out like he had seen so many times in the movies when there was a drug deal going down or when the bad guys were counting the ransom. He couldn't resist. He fanned it out under his nose, as if the scent of money satisfied all of his lust.

He opened the safe, which despite all of his travels was the only time he had ever opened a hotel safe, and stuffed all but two of the stacks inside. He set the combination and closed it shut. He double checked that it was secure.

He took the $2,600 in cash and went to the bedroom. He placed the cash on his chest and lay back on the bed and stared at the ceiling.

He thought about calling his wife to tell her. But he decided to wait. No rash judgments now. Stay calm and think. This may be my lucky trip.

He fell asleep, exhausted from the tedium that had turned to excitement with a spin of the wheel and the luck of a draw.

At about the time Dan had dozed off, Mary Roys said "I don't have any more questions."

Since the plaintiff's lawyer would not question his own expert at deposition, this concluded the proceeding. Everyone shook hands and exchanged pleasantries that none of them meant. The expert and his lawyer left right away. Mary stayed behind to gather up and reorganize all of the documents she had used throughout the deposition. She double checked with the court reporter that all the exhibits had been properly marked, and that the reporter had copies of each to attach to the transcript.

She left as the court reporter was packing up her equipment. She walked out into the blazing Nevada late afternoon sun, and pulled her car keys from her purse. Today, it would be a rare early quit.

While Dan napped and Mary drove home early, the Brit played on in the poker room. He was still on a roll and still running on a chemically induced charge. He never even thought again about the fact that his wife had never called him back. Not one, single, solitary, fleeting thought about it.

Chapter 8

The Brit's wife was finishing up her session at The Palm Beach. It was nearly midnight local London time. She gathered her things and walked through the main casino where blackjack tables and three card poker tables and roulette wheels and craps tables were in play as far as one could see.

She waved good night to the men at the bell stand. It was cool this evening, for the time of year, as she walked to the garage to get her car.

The fresh air felt good to her. Before going into the garage, she stopped and leaned back against the wall and lit a cigarette. She dragged slowly and while she exhaled she put one foot back against the wall and leaned her head back to gaze at the stars. She flicked off the ash to the sidewalk under her.

She sucked in and exhaled out. What a bloody life, she thought. What a bloody life.

She threw her cigarette butt on the pavement and stamped it out with her right foot. She grabbed a piece of chewing gum out of her purse and unwrapped it. She threw the wrapper on the ground and the piece of gum into her mouth.

She drove with all four windows down. The breeze was waking her up. Traffic was light.

She arrived back at her small flat. She suddenly felt very lonely and alone. Was she married? There was a joint bank account and a man's things in the water closet, but no real man in her life. Was she in love with something else? Was he? Was playing poker more important than everything else? Wow, she thought, fucked up.

I should have called him back, she said to herself. I wonder how long he wondered whether I would call before he forgot all about it. I wonder if he even remembers my name, the color of my eyes, the way I smell out of the shower. He probably doesn't remember any of it. Oh well, such is life. My life, anyway, she thought.

She threw her keys on the small table in the tight entrance way. She kicked off her pumps one at a time, flinging them onto the floor with her toes. She lit another cigarette and placed it in the ashtray on the coffee table while she reached around to loosen her bra and to free her large breasts. When the bra strap was undone, she let out a sigh and massaged herself where the straps had dug deep lines into her flesh. What a burden, she joked to herself; all this and not even one child to suckle.

The blinds were all drawn so she slipped her blouse over her head and sat topless on the couch puffing on her fag. She wiggled out of her skirt and sat now only in panties and the faux pearl necklace she had not yet removed.

She tried to make smoke rings, a trick she had not mastered. This amused her for quite some time and for quite a few cigarettes. She crushed out her last cigarette on top of the pile of the other butts in the ashtray. As she looked down at the ashtray she reminded herself that smoking was bad and that she really ought to quit it.

She reached for the remote and turned on the television. There was a movie on about romance, lost and found and lost again love. She poured a glass of Chablis and watched the movie, holding the glass in her left hand and twirling small circles in her hair with the right. She looked peaceful with her wine and her hair and her head cocked ever so slightly to the right. Her right leg was crossed up underneath her bottom and her left leg dangled off of the couch.

There were no lights on in the room so the flicker of the picture on the screen gave the area a strange light. From the outside it looked like the movie was of her and not on the television.

The Brit's wife watched the supporting actress with great interest. She's so beautiful, she thought. Her skin, her hair, her tanned legs, and her pert, more average sized breasts; she loved it all – the complete package. How do you get so sexy? And then she said out loud, "Shit, I'd do her."

She flipped off the television set and hit the light switch to turn on the lights for the bedroom. She brushed her teeth and she brushed her hair.

She pulled off her panties, tossed them on the floor beside the bed, and reached for her nightshirt on the nightstand. But as soon as she picked the nightshirt up she tossed it back down onto the floor beside her panties.

She lay back on the bed, turned out the light, and reached down between her legs to bring pleasure to herself. Her soft moans broke the dark silence.

Chapter 9

Mary Roys was happy for once to be home at a reasonable hour. She thought about a nap before getting ready for the annual county bar association *pro bono* fundraiser held traditionally at the Grand. She would need to leave by 6:45 to make it for the start of dinner. She planned to skip as much of the happy hour as possible.

Mary was almost 44. She started practicing law in Michigan almost twenty years ago and had moved to Las Vegas when she was 30, mostly to get away from the cold Michigan winters. She rarely kept in touch with anyone from her graduating class at Columbia University and she only had a few friends with whom she still corresponded from her law school class at NYU.

Mary started her career with lofty aspirations to make a difference, to help the little guy, to seek out justice and make sure that it was done. As with many of the lawyers with those dreams, she soon found that making a difference and helping the little guy was a rough way to go and left a lot personally and financially to be desired. Slowly but early in her career, her practice shifted to corporate defense work. It was financially rewarding and fairly stable.

It always had been. It was also becoming quite a bore.

Her annual trip to the *pro bono* dinner kept her old, youthful inner self in touch with her idealistic beginnings. She was a faithful contributor of money to the cause. But she had not really done any *pro bono* work for many years. Time was money.

Mary woke from her short nap just before 6:00. She took a quick shower and dressed in her plain black cocktail dress. She took a yogurt out of the refrigerator and ate it so she would be more able to deny the hors d'oeuvres tray at the function. She did not want to arrive hungry. She grabbed a mint from the dish by the door and popped it into her mouth as she headed out.

She dreaded the time at these events before people were seated for dinner. She abhorred small talk and even more so when it was about legal work. The worst was getting caught in a conversation with a pain in the ass lawyer who had all of those "war stories" about courtroom appearances or depositions or whatever. Gag me, she would think to herself as she politely pretended to listen.

"Hi, Mary," she heard from behind her as she picked up a glass of Pinot Noir at one of the bars.

She turned and saw someone that she knew. What a relief, she thought.

"Hey, Natalie. How are you?"

"Fine, busy but fine."

"Do you usually come to this dinner? I don't remember seeing you here last year."

"Nope. This is my first time. I got roped into it by one of the partners at our firm. His wife is on the board and he needed to use several tickets to fill a table. Don't want any empty seats, right? I heard it's an ok event, though? Is it?"

"Yeah, it's not bad. It always makes me think about more volunteer work." She sipped her wine. "But that only lasts a little while since there's hardly enough time to do the work they pay you for."

"I know. The worse the economy gets the more they expect out of you," Natalie said, and she reached for some mixed nuts from the bowl on top of one of the tall cocktail tables.

"And the less they want to pay you for it."

"Anything new happening in your world," Natalie asked to try to change the subject from work.

She put the highball glass to her lips and took a very small sip of her scotch.

"No. It's the same old same old really. What about with you?"

"I'm thinking about a game changing decision, a change of career decision." Natalie stopped to shake her cocktail and melt some ice. "It's just so hard though, you know? The fear of the unknown can be really palpable. There's a lot to be said for the old comfort zone."

"I hear ya. I could use a little excitement and change too. I'm kinda in one of those middle age funks, you know what I mean?"

Mary looked around to see if anyone was close enough to be listening.

"I'm kind of wondering what it all means and what I've added to the whole thing." She sipped her wine. "What've I been doing for 20 years?"

Natalie became animated and answered quickly, at a fast pace. "I know exactly what you mean. That is so fucking weird. You're in the "will anybody miss me when I am gone" zone. So am I."

"Exactly," Mary said. "If I choke on this canapé I'm not sure if anybody would miss me. I worry about an empty funeral home at the services for me. Do you know what I mean? Is there time to change that?"

Natalie shifted from her left foot to her right, trying not to look awkward in the crowd.

"I hope so. We all hope so. We just never seem to get around to it. Too busy to do what really matters, I guess."

"Have ya ever thought of just starting over and doing something completely different?"

"Sure, all the time. I think about writing. I think about starting a small business. I think about selling my big house and selling my nice car and moving to the Keys to sell t-shirts and conch shells and live in a small bungalow where I sip wine at night with my toes in the gulf. I think about all of that shit. But I don't have the guts. I don't have the balls. There's no getting me out of my comfort zone."

"Sucks, doesn't it." Mary looked down at her now empty wine glass. "I'm the same freaking way. I know I'm unhappy, but I'm too content to do anything about it."

Then Mary said, "And no, you don't have the balls."

They both giggled and Natalie sipped her drink. They took quick looks around the room to see who was there and what was happening. Mary thought about getting a refill on the wine, but decided against it.

"The whole unhappy and content thing; is that ironic? I always get confused about what's really ironic? I'm paranoid to use the word ironic because I might screw it up and look like an idiot. So I just never say it anymore."

Mary laughed and said, "What's ironic is that an English major from UCSD doesn't know what irony is. Irony is the difference between expectation and reality. It's ironic that the police chief robbed the bank."

She paused for a reaction.

"So, is it, you know, ironic if you're too content to deal with your unhappiness?"

"I'll be damned if I know."

Mary noticed the lights flicker.

"Finally," she said, "time to sit down."

She finished her drink.

"Time can really stand still at these things."

Mary felt bad almost instantly.

"No offense, Natalie…"

"None taken," and Natalie laughed and drained her scotch.

As they walked into the event room, they smiled at each other in mutual understanding.

"I know. Let's get a table in the back and get drunk."

After a few boring and predictable speeches that included the obligatory pleas for money, the event ended. The crowd began to filter out. Mary and Natalie worked hard to avoid the small pockets of lawyers gathered here and there talking about this or that.

"Nightcap?" asked Mary.

"Why not," Natalie agreed.

They went to the Café Allegro, which was very close to the exit. Better to have a drink than to stand in the long valet parking line.

"I'll have a Riesling," Natalie said.

"Make mine a Courvoisier," Mary said, checking her texts and emails.

"Put that thing away. There's absolutely nothing on there that can't wait until tomorrow."

"You're right. Sorry."

"Look," said Natalie as they waited for their drinks. "We're both still young and…", she was interrupted by the arrival of the drinks, served by a knockout blonde with a tight ass and huge boobs.

"Not that young," Mary said smiling as the waitress wiggled away.

"Whatever." She stopped to roll her eyes. "We're young, relatively speaking, and we deserve to do something exciting, something that will make us feel good about ourselves. What can we do?"

"I don't know. I wish I did."

Mary leaned over and put her elbows on the table. She let out a huge sigh. Natalie took another taste of the sweet wine.

Mary looked directly at Natalie and said, "But it gets harder and harder to get up and go do the same freaking thing day in and day out. We're on a wheel and we can't slow it down or get off."

They both sipped their drinks and sensed together what a downer their conversation had become.

"We're really good for each other's morale. We really need to do this more often."

They both laughed.

"Doing anything fun this weekend?" Mary broke the silence.

"Don't know yet. I heard it may get cooler."

"That'd be fine by me. I have some outside work to do and the cooler the better."

They finished their drinks and paid the tab around 10:45. Mary and Natalie exchanged goodbyes and promises to stay in touch, promises neither meant to keep.

Natalie disappeared into the ladies room.

Mary waited in line for the valet to bring her car around. While she was in line, the phone in her dark downtown office was ringing.

"Hello, you have reached the voice mail of Mary Roys. I am not able to take your call right now. Please leave a short message and I will return your call as soon as I can. Thank you. Bye."

A man with a British accent was leaving a message.

The Brit hung up the phone and turned away from the wall. He was led to a small room crowded with other men. He slinked to the corner and sat with his back against the wall. He pulled his knees to his chest and set his feet on the bench in front of him. He sobbed himself to sleep. Another man is pushed into the room, and the door is slammed shut behind him.

Chapter 10

While Mary and Natalie were having pre-dinner drinks at the *pro bono* event, the Brit was on fire. The cards were coming to him and calling to him and working for him. He had never been so lucky. He had never been so spot on with every call, every fold, for that matter with every play. He was making his monthly nut in a matter of hours. The dealer couldn't dole cards out fast enough for him. The other players were agitated and becoming suspicious. They'd never seen luck quite like this.

The security boys upstairs were growing ever more interested as well. The Brit's play was flying in the face of all normal odds. They now trained a camera solely on the Brit to watch his every move. If he was cheating, by god, they were going to get him.

The Brit had just finished off another player, opening up a seat to his right, when Dan arrived on the casino floor and asked for a seat at a table.

"We may have one for you right now, sir," the man in charge of the poker room said as he looked to make sure the player next to the Brit was leaving.

"Sure enough," he said. "Follow me."

And they walked in as the man playing next to the Brit walked out mumbling profanities.

Dan sat down and was surprised to find himself next to the Brit. The Brit was high and did not remember Dan. He decided not to remind him.

Dan had been doing some soul searching. He'd also been doing some drinking from the mini-bar in his room. He had all of the $13,000 he had just won in his pockets at the table. He had $6,500 in the left front pocket and $6,500 in the right front pocket. He pulled all of the bills out of his left pocket. He bought $6,500 in chips. Half of the money he had won was now fully at risk.

The Brit had a mountain of chips stacked in front of an equally impressive stack of $100 bills on the table before him. This guy must be really doing well since he took my $300. He's on a roll.

"Thanks everyone. Good luck," said the dealer as he showed the boys upstairs his hands, front and back, and clapped to show them he was not palming anything. A new dealer sat down, a cute redhead with a button smile. She gave everyone their cards.

The action at the table was light for the first hour or so. The redhead dealt the cards and the Brit cupped his hands to look at his draw. He had Jacks, one club one spade.

Dan looked at his cards. He had nines, one club one spade.

The Brit started the betting with a $20 raise. Three players called in front of Dan, and he did the same.

The redhead burnt a card and flopped three cards down. The flop was a three of diamonds, a nine of hearts, and a two of diamonds.

Dan had a set of nines and the Brit had a pair of Jacks. Both felt good.

The Brit bet $100. One other player before Dan called. Dan raised the bet to $200. The Brit looked at him cockeyed but without much hesitation called. The other player folded. It was head to head.

The redhead smiled and put a card face down in the burn pile and one face up as the turn. The Brit was amazed. It was the Jack of hearts. Damn, he thought to himself, this is too easy. I could get used to this shit.

He checked to entice Dan to bet. Give him enough rope to let him hang himself, the Brit thought. Nice and easy, mate, keep taking the bait. His mind flashed to passages from *The Old Man and the Sea* where the old man was begging the big fish to take the fresh bait on his sharpened hook. Oxford wasn't a complete waste, he thought.

Dan was calmed by the alcohol and was not giving away his three nines by any outward emotion or display. He thought a long time before betting. He rattled a small stack of chips in his right hand. He counted out various assortments and stacks of chips signaling to the Brit that it was not a matter of whether he was going to bet, but only a matter of how much. The Brit was content with this show of bravado and wished it to keep going.

Dan sat back and leaned as if to stretch before lifting the massive bet to the middle of the table. He sighed out loud as he stared at the little black Plexiglas bubble that was staring back down at him. He took a sip of water and deliberately placed the cap back on it. He finally settled on the amount of his bet and pushed out $1,000.

This gave the Brit pause. Well, well, well, he thought. Have I run into a set? It can't be bigger than mine. Is he chasing a straight draw with such a big bet here? I don't know and I guess I don't care. He raised the bet to $5,000 and without flinching Dan called.

Now the Brit was paranoid. What had me missed? Was this bloke flipping crazy? What a major league freaking bluff if that's what it is, mind you, a real major league move.

The Brit felt perspiration under the collar of his shirt and that clammy feeling on his hands. His tongue was sticking to the roof of his mouth and he thought of the movie *Jaws* when Hooper says "I got no spit." He was feeling dizzy. Don't let it be over, sweet mother of Jesus don't let it be over.

The Brit studied Dan, who seemed to be much calmer than he was and this positively scared the shit out of him. Please let this hand be over and please let me rake these chips in and please make my pile bigger and his smaller and please oh please oh please.

The redhead burnt one more card as the other eight players leaned in now over the table since this was the biggest pot any of them had seen at this table all day. The hand was even getting some attention from other tables as the word spread around that a mighty big pot was up for a head to head battle.

The river: the nine of diamonds. Dan had scored the four of a kind. He nearly fell out of his chair. He struggled to remain calm as his insides were shaking and his heart was pounding. Dan knew that he had won. The only hands that could beat a four of a kind are the royal flush and the straight flush and neither was remotely possible with what was on the table before him. There could not be a higher card four of a kind. He had won, and the Brit would be drawing dead, no card could save him.

But it was not over yet. The Brit was excited to see the nine. He was hoping that this had given his opponent three of them. That might keep him in to battle against the Brit's set of Jacks.

The bet was to the Brit and he would milk every drop of drama out of the moment. He was confident. The sweat had stopped, his mouth was moist again. He had an erection. Uncharacteristically, he did not even for a second consider an opponent with four of the nines.

Badly mistaken about his opponent's hand, the Brit was savoring the moment. He would torture Dan. He would make him wait. He would make him sweat and have his mouth go dry. The power was palpable and the Brit did not want to surrender it.

"You've presented a very strong hand throughout, mate. Really have me stymied, I must say. It's quite a bit of a decision, isn't it? I mean a lot of money on the table and a bit rough to just walk away from it without a go at it, eh? They do call it gambling don't they? I suppose once in a while you've got to take a flyer when you're gambling."

He flipped his yellow chips confidently.

"Mate, I have come along away across the ocean blue to play cards and play cards I will. I am, mate, nothing less than all in."

Dan almost pissed himself. And with that the Brit sat back with a mile wide shit eating grin.

Dan was paralyzed with happiness and could not move or speak. He was moments away from doubling his money. It would not take the Brit out, but it would deal him a crushing blow – literally and figuratively. He composed himself.

The boys on the catwalk and in the control room with all the monitors were all focused on the action between Dan and the Brit. If this sucker was cheating he would not let this hand get away.

"I call."

Before Dan could turn over his cards the Brit turned over his Jacks. There were gasps and grunts and expletives and high fives and oh shits going around. As the Brit, face flushed and smiling wide, moved his arms in to embrace the chips Dan said in uncharacteristic and nasty fashion "Not so fast partner." And he threw out his pocket nines with the flourish of a matador nearing the kill.

"Look at the four of a kind, my friend. Look at the four of a kind."

The other eight players were beside themselves. The excitement spread through the whole room. Amidst it all was the Brit. He was ashen grey.

"It's not right," he muttered. "It's bloody wrong, is what it is."

He buried his head in his hands on the table as the dealer counted Dan's chips to assess the Brit what he owed.

Sheepishly the Brit passed over the piles of chips that Dan had acquired from him in this massive showdown.

"Don't let this be the start," the Brit whispered. "Please don't let this be the start."

In a matter of minutes his fortune had been halved and that of Dan had been doubled.

The Brit went to the bathroom and sat down in the handicapped stall on the toilet. He was fully dressed and the pee from the previous patron soaked through his trousers. He started to cry quietly and then to sob uncontrollably. He stammered over and over "I get it but I can't keep it."

The Brit sat on the john for a long time.

He got up and dried off the back of his pants with some paper towels and he washed his hands with soap and very hot water, disgusted with his condition in general. He splashed cold water on his face and marched back to the table.

The Brit could not focus. He meandered through a few hands, making several amateur mistakes. Dan was less aggressive and happy to fondle the large number of chips in front of him. The Brit thought a nap was in order to clear his head. He cashed out at the cashier's window and walked slowly to his room.

He did not undress or even empty his pockets. He flopped onto the bed face down and fell into a fitful sleep almost right away.

Chapter 11

The Brit was asleep for only about an hour. When he woke he was depressed. He took four little white pills out of his pocket and went to the mini-bar. He took out two small vodka bottles from the shelf in the refrigerator and poured them both into the water glass on the table. He popped all of the pills into his mouth and gulped a large swig of vodka to wash them down. He sat still as if to wait for the pills to jolt him to life.

When the Brit returned to the table he had all of his remaining cash with him. He was not thinking clearly. The pills and the vodka, which he had supplemented with two more small bottles before leaving his room, were definitely affecting his ability to process information. His mind was racing. He decided that he needed to blitzkrieg the table, a full out frontal assault. He was charged up and over the top with false confidence.

Dan was still playing.

When Dan saw the Brit sitting down he said "Hey, sorry about before. I got excited and I was a prick. Really, no shit, I was way out of line; my apologies."

The Brit did not look at him and nodded an acknowledgement.

Dan did not push it.

The cards were dealt again and again. All the while, the Brit tossed his two yellow chips back and forth from one hand to the other. His eyes darted back and forth from the cards on the table to the faces of the players. He was fidgety, impatient, out of sorts.

"Let's play mates," the Brit said. "We're all here to play so let's have at it, shall we?"

It was nearly 9:30.

The Brit was edgy. "Hurry up with my drink," he said to the cocktail waitress. He was no longer a polite Englishman. "Hurry up, I said. I'm parched."

The dealer intervened, "You're getting close to over the line. If you want to stay and play you better tone it down."

The Brit, fearful of being taken out of the action, took the message and tried to control himself. He apologized to the waitress, "Sorry, love. A bit out of sorts I guess, no harm meant. Take your time. I'll be all right."

She returned with his drink and he flipped a $5 dollar chip on her tray to smooth things over. The Brit took a large swallow of vodka. "I need a hand to play, mates. I want a hand to play."

At 9:37 the Brit got two nines. He played it. The betting went round and round until he found himself all in against Dan again. Everything he had, everything, was in the middle of the table. He was heads up against the same stranger who had beaten him earlier in a monumental showdown.

He wanted to grab the chips back and he wanted to say I was only kidding and he wanted to curl up under the table and go to sleep, caressing the chips gently. He could do none of these things now. He was all in.

He lost.

"Are you all right, sir?" the dealer said looking at the Brit.

The Brit's eyes glazed over. He sat motionless for what seemed like hours. He watched Dan rake the large pile of chips.

"Hey, man, tough hand," said the player to his right. "You win that one 99 percent of the time. That's really shitty luck, my friend. Sorry."

The Brit showed no sign of responding.

Dan was getting several trays to cash out. He was ecstatic but he was keeping it to himself because it was easy for him to see that this development had crushed the Englishman. He would celebrate later but not in front of this man. He genuinely felt sorry for him.

The Brit's hands were shaking now as he tried to lift the glass to his mouth for the last bit of vodka. He spilled some down his chin and drained the glass.

Dan was gone, and the Brit spied him leaving toward the elevators.

The Brit pushed himself up and swayed until he could get his legs underneath and establish some balance. He walked in a slightly serpentine line out of the poker room and toward the elevators. He put a hand in each empty pocket.

He was starting to cry. He wiped his eyes and saw Dan heading for the bank of elevators for floors 30-39. He stumbled close enough to Dan's car to see that he pushed the button 34. As the doors closed, the Brit quickly pushed the up button and boarded the next car. He pushed 34.

The hallways in the hotel were very long and the elevators were all the way to one end. The Brit disembarked on the 34th floor and bounded around the corner to catch a glimpse of Dan, who had a decent head start of about 20 yards. The Brit stayed quiet and kept his distance. Dan approached his room and without turning or looking back fanned the electronic key over the sensor and opened the door and went in.

The Brit knew there were surveillance cameras everywhere, even in the hotel hallways, so he kept his cool. He kept walking past the room which Dan had entered and paced steadily all the way to the end of the hall where he stopped as if to look out the large window. He took out his cell phone and pretended to make a call. He held the phone to his ear while his mind raced.

He gestured as if he was talking to someone on the phone. He was thinking.

The Brit ended his phony call and put the phone into his jacket pocket. He ran his right hand through his hair. He scratched the back of his neck. He wiped across his mouth. He walked back down the hallway.

"Hotel security," he said in his best American accent.

He knocked on Dan's door again.

"Hotel security."

Dan had already partially undressed when he heard the door and the announcement. He put on gym shorts and a t-shirt and went to the door.

"Hold on. I'm coming."

Dan tried to look through the peep hole but the Brit had side stepped the door so Dan could not see. Misjudging the situation, Dan cracked the door open and the Brit slammed it in against him, knocking Dan back off of his feet. The Brit stepped in quickly and closed the door behind.

"Easy, mate," he said in his native accent. "Don't be alarmed. I just need a minute with you. There's nothing to fret about really, nothing to fret about at all, alright?"

"What the fuck is this?" Dan yelled. "Get the fuck out of here."

"Easy now," and as he said this he punched Dan hard in the solar plexus with the heel of his open palm. Dan gasped and went to his knees. While Dan struggled for breath the Brit bound Dan's hands crudely with Dan's computer cord that was on the table. He grabbed a wash cloth and shoved it into Dan's mouth so he could not scream.

The Brit pushed Dan into the small bathroom that was close to the front door of the room and he closed the bathroom door to further insulate Dan from the hallway.

The Brit started to frantically look through the room for the cash. He was panicked and drunk and high and he was not finding the money.

In the meantime, Dan had crawled to the phone in the bathroom and with his head pushed the handset off of the cradle. He used his nose to hit 0 for the hotel operator. He could hear the feint voice of the operator as he lay on the floor with his hands tied and his mouth gagged.

"This is the front desk. Hello. This is the hotel operator, how can I help you? Hello? Is everything alright?"

Dan pounded his forehead on the table next to the phone's mouthpiece as hard as he could to signal that something was wrong. He pushed numbers on the key pad with his nose to make sure the operator knew someone was there, someone who was not able to speak.

"Hello. Is everything alright? Hello. If you can hear me I'm sending security right now. I'll stay on the line."

The door to the bathroom flung open.

"Alright, mate. Where is it? I just need a little back so I can get back in the game. You understand? You'll still be a big winner. But you see I have a sickness. I can't not play, mate. And I can't play without money – and you have all my money. Am I being clear? I need some of the money back. You can't have it all. Where the fuck is the money?"

While the Brit was talking and pacing and foaming at the mouth, Dan was slowly loosening the wire around his hands. As he surreptitiously worked his hands free he never took his eyes off of the Brit.

"Come on, lad. Time is wasting and time is money. Give me back a measly $1,000 and you keep the rest. You promise to forget about this little intrusion and I'll give you half of what I win with the $1,000."

The Brit was short of breath. He had just now considered how he could not get away with this. He was working on a way out, and he lost all focus on the man he had hit, bound, and gagged.

"Look. I lost my senses here. Let me untie you. Insane, really, don't you think? Don't know what I was thinking. Let's have a drink and sort this out…"

In the middle of the Brit's plea Dan made himself loose from the cord tied around his wrists. He swung both of his fists across the Brit's face and landed a good, hard blow. The Brit reeled around and fell halfway down. He instinctually grabbed the lamp on the table beside the door and brought it down on Dan's head. It happened so fast.

Dan went limp. A pool of blood was forming around his head on the tile floor. The Brit was sitting on the floor with the lamp in his lap and his hand on his jaw which Dan had badly bruised.

"My god," the Brit whispered. "Oh, my god."

The Brit dragged Dan back into the bathroom and shoved him into the far corner. He grabbed a towel from the rack. He wiped off the lamp very carefully. He wiped off every area in the room that he could remember touching. He took one last quick look around for the money. He saw a pair of trousers folded over the valet near the foot of the bed. He rifled through the pockets. Nothing.

He glanced back in to see if Dan was moving. He noticed the phone off of the hook and with the towel in his hand he picked it up.

"What's going on in there? Help's on the way. Help's on the way."

The Brit said "shit" and shook his head. He hung up the phone.

Hotel security arrived as he was wiping off the door handle.

Chapter 12

The ambulance pulled to the front of the hotel and the paramedics wheeled the stretcher through the wide corridor between the blackjack and three card poker tables. They waited with everyone else for the elevator.

The paramedics, with their stretcher and medical kits, boarded the elevator and headed for the 34th floor. They got off of the elevator and started the long walk down the hallway to Dan's room. There was a lot of commotion in the hall; police, hotel security, other guests popping out of rooms to see what was happening. Coming the other way, escorted by police, was a man in a red sport coat. He was in handcuffs and he walked with his head down, looking at his feet. The paramedics passed opposite the man and the police in silence.

Dan was taken out of his hotel room with an IV dripping into his right arm and with an oxygen mask over his nose and mouth. He was wheeled unceremoniously past gamblers, hookers, and gawkers. The lights flashing on top of the ambulance were absorbed by the surrounding neon and did not make much of a difference in the overall lighting in front of the building.

The paramedics lifted the stretcher into the back of the van and one paramedic jumped in the back and the other took her position behind the wheel. The ambulance pulled around the cul de sac and headed toward the crowded strip. The driver turned on the siren and tried as best as she could to navigate through the heavy traffic. Time was of the essence and it seemed to take an inordinate amount of time to make any progress down the heavily congested street.

The driver glanced in the rear view mirror and saw her partner monitoring Dan's pulse and blood pressure.

"He's hanging in there," a voice came from the back, barely audible over the siren.

"We'll be there in about ten minutes," the driver replied. "They're ready for him."

The ambulance was in front of the ER entrance now and the paramedics rushed Dan into examination room 3. The doctor examined the patient for the first time.

"OK. His pressure's not bad. We need to maintain perfusion. Let's get some normotonic fluids started. Take that blanket off of him," the doctor was in charge and forcefully barking orders.

"He's going to the OR as soon as possible so let's get a tube in him just in case. It won't cause any harm and they can take it out there if they don't agree," she said as she saw Dan struggling to breathe.

"Doc, neurology is on the phone," said one of the nurses.

"I'll take it over here. Keep an eye on him," she said as she stepped out for some privacy.

The neurosurgeon spoke first, "What's the volume of the hemorrhage doctor?" he asked.

"It looks like just around 4 cm and we may have a structural vascular lesion. They are taking him for the CT now so we'll know more in about 15 minutes."

The CT scan showed a somewhat larger bleed than the ER doctor had expected so surgery was the definite next step for Dan. In the corner a nurse was going through Dan's wallet, which the paramedics had picked up in his room and brought along for identification of the patient and for trying to contact next of kin. She found his Kentucky driver's license and gave it to an attendant.

"Go see what you can find out from this," she said, handing him the license. "We need to try to contact family. This is touch and go."

The attendant hurried off to contact the police and to begin with her own Google searches. Google will be faster, she thought to herself.

The surgery took almost three hours.

Dan had tubes and wires running into him all over the place when he was placed in the bed in the ICU. His breathing was easier through the tube. His color was bad and his right hand twitched every so often. His eyelids fluttered but never opened. He was either fast and deeply asleep, or in a coma.

The nurse on rounds noted on his chart that Dan was a little red in the face, a change from the previous observation of pale and grey skin color. His temperature was 99.1, close enough to normal. He appeared to this nurse to be resting in no acute distress.

The ICU was very quiet, with an eerie glow from the medical devices and instruments surrounding and connected to the people in the beds.

Sweat was forming on Dan's upper lip as he slept through the night. His face got redder and his left leg started to swell.

At 6:32 a.m. Dan was pronounced dead. The doctor noted the cause of death as pulmonary embolism secondary to cerebral hemorrhage caused by blunt trauma to the head.

At 9:54 Eastern Time the phone rang in Dan's kitchen in Kentucky. Dan's wife, Patti, was coming in from the garage and rushed to get the phone. She was out of breath.

"Hello," she said. But she was too late. The caller had hung up. She put the phone down and went back to the garage to finish cleaning out the freezer. While she was in the garage the message light started to flash on the phone. She could not see it.

Patti was preoccupied this morning. She was five days late for her period and she was starting to think that maybe she was finally pregnant. She did not want to take the home pregnancy test without Dan at home. She was chomping at the bit to know, though, and she could not wait to talk to him.

A little after 11:00 in the morning Patti came in to get a glass of water. She saw the message light. She picked up the phone and pressed the buttons until she landed on "Listen to New Messages." She clicked on it.

"One new message," said the robotic voice. "Playing new message… beep," came through the earpiece.

She called right away to the number the Las Vegas police department had left on her machine. She was panicking. This could not be good.

"Hello. Las Vegas police department, how may I direct your call?"

"This is Patti Berry from Kentucky and I am returning a message from about an hour or so ago."

The person on the line from Las Vegas scanned the notepad in front of her and she read the message that had been hurriedly scribbled for her: When Mrs. Berry calls put her right through to me. Lenny.

"Yes, Mrs. Berry. Please hold while I connect you."

It seemed to Patti like she was on hold forever.

Finally, a voice came on the line, "Mrs. Berry?"

"Yes, this is Mrs. Berry. Who is this?"

"Mrs. Berry, this is Detective Leonard Small with the Las Vegas police department."

Her heart jumped into her throat. She sat down involuntarily at the kitchen table. She dropped the glass of water she had been holding and it crashed onto the acrylic counter top.

"What's wrong?" she said.

"I have bad news Mrs. Berry. I'm very sorry to have to tell you over the phone. Your husband Dan is dead. He's been murdered."

The detective heard the phone hit the floor. Patti had feinted.

"Hello. Mrs. Berry are you there, ma'am. Mrs. Berry, please say something. Are you alright?"

Getting no response he put the call on hold and used another line to call the local police in Kentucky and asked them to send a car around right away to the Berry residence.

The County deputy sheriff screeched the patrol car to a stop in front of the Berry's house. The deputy jumped out of the car and ran to the front door. He looked in through the window next to the door and saw a pretty woman kneeling on the kitchen floor, sobbing uncontrollably. He knocked several times but it was apparent that she did not hear or did not care. He turned the door knob and found that it was open. He opened the door, walked slowly to the kitchen, and knelt next to Mrs. Berry. He put his hand on her shoulder gently and said very softly "I'm so sorry Mrs. Berry. I'm so dang sorry. God bless, I'm sorry."

She fell flat to the floor and continued to cry. The Deputy Sheriff sat next to her on the floor, tears welling up in his eyes and his left fist clenching at his side.

Chapter 13

News of Dan Berry's death hit like a tidal wave in Bromley. At the diner, regulars at the lunch counter talked about nothing else.

"Poor son of a bitch."

"I know, a man goes on a little business trip and don't come home."

"I hear it was a foreign dude that done it."

"Fuck."

"Figures."

"And I hear that his wife just found out she's pregnant. Right after she got the news about him being dead and all."

"That truly sucks. That really sucks."

"Damn shame."

"Wish I could get my hands on that foreign son of a bitch and show him what for Kentucky style."

"Ain't that the truth."

And it went on.

One man listening but not talking was Jimmy Gatlin. Jimmy grew up in Bromley and knew just about everyone in it. He was shocked at the news.

The other guys at the counter kept speculating about what had happened. The church going faction blamed it on the decadence and sin in Las Vegas. What did he expect; he should have never gone in the first place. The boozing and sexing and crystal meth rednecks talked about how to exact revenge, whether women were involved, and things of that sort. The hybrids, which were the majority, did both.

Finally, Jimmy spoke up "I never been very far from this here county let alone to Las Vegas but it seems to me it don't matter where a man goes. Nothing like this should happen to a good feller anywhere, no how." He spit into an empty pop bottle with an inch or two of black residue at the bottom. He went on "Mr. Berry was a right nice guy, with a right nice wife, and what looked to me to be a right nice future. Now this guy out there in Las Vegas done took all that from him." He spit again, and wiped his lips on his sleeve. "Don't any of you see how truly fucked up it is?"

They were surprised. Jimmy rarely said anything and this amounted to the biggest speech that any of them could ever remember. They were quiet.

Jimmy did not wait for an answer. He picked up his baseball cap and put it on his head. He spit again into the bottle and set it down on the counter next to his empty coffee cup. He turned to walk out and as he left they heard him say "shit." The bell on the door clanged as he slammed it behind him.

Chapter 14

The Brit's wife got out of bed on Thursday morning at around 9:45. She darted up and into the shower because this morning was a big morning for her. She had decided to go to a therapist for counseling. She'd done this on her own; no one else knew. She'd been thinking about doing it for some while but had found reason after reason to put it off.

"It's really poppy cock," she would tell herself. Or, "I surely can't afford to pay someone just to listen to me. Can't I find that for free somewhere," and she would laugh to herself.

But it had gotten bad. Her marriage was a mess. Her life was a mess. She felt that she was truly at a crossroads; she cringed at thinking of her life in terms of such on overdone expression. But it fit.

She turned the shower on and while the water was heating up she brushed her teeth, spitting into the sink and noticing a bit of pink in her pasty saliva. "I need to see the dentist," she thought, and then quickly reminded herself, "but there's only enough for one professional at a time, so for now the therapy trumps the dentistry." And she watched the spittle go down the drain with just a little bit of her blood in it.

She showered quickly and dried herself while sipping the cup of tea she had brewed. Edith didn't eat breakfast very often, a habit she kept from her childhood. Tea and a cigarette were plenty to get her started.

She dressed in her best dress jeans and a top she had bought just for this occasion. It was conservative and she looked in the mirror and approved to herself of what she saw. She made one last go over to make sure everything worked. She checked her hair and her lipstick and her makeup and her jeans to make sure they did not make her butt look big. When she was finished with her final inspection, she picked up her purse and headed out the door.

The bus made its way through the mid-week, mid-morning London traffic. She lived in the neighborhood known as Bloomsbury and the therapist was close by in the next neighborhood to the northeast, Clerkenwell. The bus ride only took about 15 minutes.

She got off at the corner just past the small row of offices where the therapist she had found on a chat page was located. She glanced at her watch. She was just a minute or two late but not bad off at all. She walked briskly to the offices at 11333 Marlboro Way and went through the double front doors. She looked over the office directory behind the glass on the wall in the small lobby.

Her eyes glanced quickly over the list in alphabetical order until she got to the L's: Larrimor, Dennis; Lorne, Harvey, ah, there it is, she said to herself, Lunat, Ivan. She noted that Lunat's office was on the 4th floor and she went straight to the lift.

Ivan Lunat was a certified and licensed therapist but not a psychiatrist or psychologist. She had chosen this level of professional expertise with due deliberation. First, she had concluded that she was not crazy. She was making this decision to try therapy only because she needed to open up to someone who knew how to listen and who could maybe help get her life back on the rails. And second, who was she kidding, she couldn't afford anything more. Lunat charged 45 pounds for an hour session.

The Brit's wife opened the door that had Lunat's name stenciled on smoked glass. He was a solo practitioner so it was a small shop. There was no receptionist. There was a small desk with a sign-in pad and a few chairs configured around a small coffee table with magazines and newspapers. In the corner there was a small station for tea and a water cooler.

She signed her maiden name, Edith Hatcher, and the time of her arrival. At the top of the sheet it said, "Please sign in and take a seat in the waiting area. I will be with you as soon as the current session ends. Thank you."

She was about to sit down when she was startled by a voice from behind her. "Hello. I'm Ivan Lunat. Welcome. Won't you please come in," and he gestured her through the door he was holding open into his small office. She nodded her head politely and nervously and walked through the door as he smiled at her.

Lunat was in his mid-40's and in reasonably good shape. He was average looking and his hairline was receding just a bit. His skin was olive and he did not appear to be a native of the British Isles. The Brit's wife couldn't really conclude as to any particular nationality other than it was not British. He didn't waste a lot of time, which she appreciated. She was especially glad that he did not look creepy, which was her biggest fear before setting foot into his office.

"Alright," he said. "I know you're probably anxious…" and he stopped and smiled. "No, sorry, I mean eager to begin."

"Yes, actually I am. It's a rather big financial decision to be doing this so the more we can accomplish with our time the better."

"Right, I completely understand. Then let's have at it. It's really most helpful for me if I can spend at least half of our first hour learning just a little bit about your background. It seems that's always the most effective and efficient way to start. OK"?

"Yes," she said. "I actually expected that."

"Good," he said. "So let's get started. Do you want any water or anything like that?"

"No, thank you though. I'm fine."

"Tea?"

"No, really, I'm quite alright."

"OK. First off, did you grow up in London?"

"No," she said. "I grew up in Leeds."

And she started to explain to Lunat about some of her earliest years there. He took a lot of notes. One of them was that she did not look at him when she talked.

"How did you get along with your parents, your family, that kind of thing?"

She paused for a long time. "Not very well," she finally said and for the first time she looked to him to be nervous.

"Can you tell me more?"

"I don't know where to start really."

"Well, let me help you, ok? Let's talk about your mother first."

"OK. Let me think a second," and she paused to reflect. She went on, "My mother had no time to be a mother. She worked all the time to try to make enough money to pay the rent and to put food on the table for me and my two younger sisters." She stopped to fidget. "I guess she just never had time to do the other things mothers do with their kids." She paused again and he did not say anything. "She did the best she could with the hand she was dealt."

"How about your father?"

She bit her lower lip.

"Can you tell me a little about him?"

The question about her father struck a chord and he could tell.

"My father was home almost all of the time because he was out of work for most of my life," she said first. "I remember when I was very young he had a job at the fabric mill but the mill was shut down and he lost the job. From that point he was home. I don't remember him ever looking for any other work. I remember he sat by the phone and drank. He drank beer in the morning and he switched to gin or vodka by mid-afternoon. If the phone rang he answered it, a lot of the time slurring his words, depending on what time the call came in. No one else was allowed to answer the phone if he was in the flat. He always thought the call was for him to go back to the mill."

Lunat was taking notes. She stopped talking. After an appropriate pause he felt it necessary to prod her along.

"So how did this affect the rest of you?"

"My mum simply took over for us. Dad got a little public assistance but not nearly enough to keep four people fed and warm and clothed. Mum started to clean houses for other people while our house got dirty and she did laundry for other people while our clothes piled up on the bedroom floors. She did what she had to do to make ends meet."

He didn't say anything when she stopped. The pen he held to his notepad indicated that he wanted her to go on.

"When I was old enough, and my sisters too when they were old enough, picked up the slack at home. While my mum worked outside of the house to bring home a little money, we kept the house, working around my father. He was the fixture by the phone in the middle of the sitting room."

This time when she paused he interjected.

"How did you and your sisters get along with that?" he asked. "With your mother gone and the three of you at home with him, I mean."

His pen was always taking something down even when he was asking her something.

"I told you before, and I'm not exaggerating, dad drank most of the time he was awake. He for sure drank up most of the money that came in from the government. My sisters and I ignored him. He was like furniture. He did not really bother us, or bother with us for that matter. It felt like we should run the vacuum over him. Like we should dust around his head and wipe behind his knees. That was it."

Lunat glanced at his watch hoping that she would not notice. They better move on, he thought.

"OK. Let's spend some time on you now. That's why we're here after all, right?" and he smiled to try to put her at ease. "How did you like school?"

She was quick to answer, "I went because I had to. I never cared for it and I never saw any usefulness in it for the long run. It did give me time away from the flat, though, and for that I was grateful."

She looked up at the ceiling. He noticed that a small smile was developing. He left her for a moment with her thoughts.

"When I was just about 7 or so I was quite the tomboy. I didn't play with dolls or have little tea parties or fancy myself dressed like a lady with a parasol and a beautiful bonnet. Far from all of that, I liked to play football in the alley with my boy mates. I was a much better player than the boys. I mean, really, I kicked ass in that alley. I scored the goals and when we needed to protect a lead I stood in goal to block shots."

Lunat looked up briefly from his notepad to ask, "Why do you bring that up?"

"I guess for background for when we get to my marriage."

"Really?"

"Yes. I guess it was my first experience in the battle of the sexes."

"How so?"

"I learned that if I wanted to keep playing with the boys I'd better tone down my game. My athletic superiority was putting the little bastards off. I intentionally underplayed so the little boy, soon to be little man, egos weren't bruised. It was the only way I could assure they wouldn't exclude me from the games."

"Interesting."

"It also came up again much later and showed me that men think they know everything."

"When was that? What happened?"

"A few months before I met my husband I was dating this guy who was studying psychology at King's College..."

"Very good school," he interjected. "Sorry, please go on."

"This guy psychoanalyzed everything. It really was a bore." She hadn't meant to insult Lunat. "Oh my, no offense," she said.

"I have a thicker skin that that," and he put on a wry smile.

She continued, "So one night at dinner we're talking about our childhood memories and silly stuff like that and the football thing comes up, just like I told it to you pretty much, ok? And he starts in with this bullshit about how early masculine-type gender-role behavior influences this that and the other thing. I remember the words he used exactly because I couldn't believe his bullshit. He starts with the Freud on a date for Christ's sake."

She smiled. She did not seem angry.

"It was our last date."

He smiled too. He waited for a moment to see if she was finished.

She seemed as if she would move on to another topic, but then she hesitated. "One more thing I guess. How are we for time?"

"We're good. Please go on."

"During one of the football games, when I had just turned 8 years old, the ball skipped from the alley into the street. I was always the one who had to chase down the loose balls so I darted after it. I never saw it coming. I still can't when I remember it now ever see it coming. But I was hit by a motor scooter. They told me after that the scooter was going way too fast and that the rider had been drinking. The rider flew head over handlebars after hitting me and broke his neck when he slammed into the door of a parked car. He was killed, I was badly hurt."

"That must've been awful. Tell me how that made you feel."

"Not a lot else to tell. I play it back some time, less now than when I was younger. Did I look before I went into the street? Stuff like that."

He looked at her but did not speak.

"I had to stay at home for six months. I was plopped down in the living room next to my dad and it was like we were matching pieces." She smiled. "At least I got some time off from cleaning house."

"What did you do laid up next to your father all day?"

"Not much. I read some. But mostly I watched out the window at the boys playing football down in the alley. I remember being so sad, even crying sometimes if I knew my dad was asleep, because it seemed like the boys didn't miss me at all."

"Did you rejoin the boys when you were mended?"

"Not really. It seemed like the timing was bad. By the time I was fit and right again the boys had moved to an age where girls weren't welcome in the game, even tomboys. You know, that period where they think they hate all girls but their little hormones are charging up to lust after them like lunatics?"

"Right. Know that well enough with two boys of my own. So what did you do to take up the slack?"

"Well, nothing much for a while. The next thing I remember that caught my fancy was when I was just coming up on 11 years old. My school had an afternoon music program and I started to play the piano. I didn't have a piano at home, of course, and my time to play was limited. That made it more special."

"Did you enjoy it?"

"Very much, yes I did. And they told me I was quite good. I didn't know if that was true or if they were blowing smoke up my ass but I do know that it gave me a sense of purpose, and a kind of inner peace that I had not known up to that point, you know? I couldn't find that feeling anywhere else."

"How do you mean?"

"Well, I mean I was making something. These sounds were from me. They weren't anyone else's. It sounds weird, I know, but I felt like I owned something for the first time in my life. I fucking owned my music and no one could take it or copy it or spit on it or mock it. It was mine. Oh gosh, so sorry about the naughty language. Quite inappropriate."

"No, no problem. Please go on."

"My music got me through several years of pretty hard times."

"Do you still play?"

"No. I haven't played since I left primary school. When I left that program I lost my piano. I was very sad. And I remember feeling so guilty and ashamed because I loved the piano more than I loved anything or anybody. I loved it more than my father for sure, but that didn't cause me too much trouble. But when I thought about how I loved the piano more than I loved my mother or either of my sisters I remember feeling like a bad person. I remember thinking one night while I was awake in bed, why does my piano have to be gone and they're all still around?"

"Have you ever thought of playing again now that you are older?"

"No."

Lunat looked again at his watch. "We're really doing great. Did anything replace the piano?"

"Well, I had all this time now that I used to use in the later afternoon for my music lessons. I didn't do much of anything with that time at first. Then one day I was passing the public library. I decided to go in for at least a warm place to sit. I wasn't really interested in books but I never realized until I went in that the library has other stuff to read. So I started to read the magazines I found there. I mean I read magazines from America and from other parts of Europe. I read anything unless it was serious. I read fashion magazines, travel magazines, and gossip magazines. I started to think about what it must be like to be a movie star, surrounded by fans and adoration and with more money than you could imagine or spend. I pretended to be a rock star, playing my piano for thousands of fans in large, important venues. I fantasized about long, lush vacations in Europe, riding in the first class cars of the TGV and all of that. I guess the magazines taught me how to dream."

"Did you ever branch out beyond reading the magazines?"

"Not on purpose. But I remember one special visit to the library. It was in winter and it was very cold. I went in thinking I would look for a travel magazine where I could dream of being on a hot beach with the sun blazing down on me. I used to go to the same table in the corner of the first floor of the library, you know where the periodicals and magazines are, and that's mostly where I stayed. Usually, there were no serious books or readers over in that corner. But before I could get to the magazine rack, I noticed a book on the table. There was no one seated there so someone had left it without re-shelving it. Normally, I would've ignored it. I don't know why but this time I didn't. I picked it up. It was a book of poems by Emily Dickinson. I had some vague recollection of hearing her name somewhere from school, but I really didn't know her."

She paused and he let her take a mental break.

"So I sat down with this book, a real book, and I started to read. I read a few poems. I remember being surprised. I kept reading and then I came to a poem called *A Door Just Opened on a Street*. Do you know it?"

"No, I'm afraid not. But I promise I will read it."

"OK. So I sit there and I read it. Something clicks. I remember reading it again. Then, I just remember reading it over and over until I started to cry. I had a piece of paper in my pocket and I took it out. I was still crying. I went to the desk and borrowed a pen and I scribbled on the paper: How could anyone know? How could so few words describe my life?"

"Had you ever done that before? Make notes like that I mean?"

"Never. And I don't think I ever have since. I still have that piece of paper."

"It meant that much to you, eh?"

"Yeah, it did. I wanted to meet this Emily Dickinson. I know now that she died in 1886. I found that out when I looked into seeing if I could find her. How funny is that? How ignorant was I?"

"Not at all," Lunat said. "My goodness, not at all."

"When I realized I couldn't meet her, I decided I wanted to put down words like she did. From that point on, I loved poetry. And I don't remember ever reading a magazine in the library again. I'm not a thief, but I stole that Emily Dickinson book. It's the only thing I've stolen in my entire life."

She looked down at her feet.

With her head still down she went on, "Around that time I started a journal with my own poems. I tried for the perfection, the precision with words, that Dickinson showed me. I have, mind you, never come close. And I've never shown that journal to a living soul. And on my life I never will."

He was writing furiously on the notepad now.

When his pen stopped he asked, "Did you think about university, now that you had this interest in poetry and writing?"

"No," and she half laughed.

"What's funny?"

He was getting more interested and less worried about when the hour would end.

"Besides reading poetry at the library I also started to listen to music. We didn't have any way to play music at home, so when I found out you could do that at the library I was like a kid in the candy store. I started to explore it all. Anyway, I know we're running short on time so if it's alright I'll cut to the chase with this university thing. Is that ok?"

"Don't worry about the time."

"OK, so I am listening to all kind of stuff and I pop up on this guy Frank Zappa from America. I start to listen to his music and it really wigs me out. So I start to read about him. I find out he wrote classical music in high school, that he taught himself how to play the guitar, and that he played in an R & B band. I get really interested in this guy. I can't define his music. Sometimes it's rock, sometimes jazz, electronic, sometimes it's orchestral, I mean it's all over the place. He is drop dead serious about music. I mean, it's the guy's entire life but he makes fun of it, especially pop music. He really had an impact on me."

"What do you think made him so interesting to you?"

"I guess because he had such a quirky sense of humor. He makes fun of psychedelic music and rock opera, and especially disco. It's awesome."

"You said he had an impact on you. How so?"

"I start to look up to this guy, get really into how he thinks. I find out he's very anti-organized religion and he's very much against traditional education. So I read something that he said, and it becomes my mantra."

"I can't wait to hear."

"Zappa says – "If you want to get laid go to college, if you want an education go to the library.""

"Wow. OK, so what do you do with that?"

"I take it literally. From around 18 I start hanging around at the University of Leeds. I figure I can meet some nice young guys, satisfy my urges, and maybe meet up with an up and comer who is a keeper. I figured it was one of the best schools in England and the prospects for an easy life by marrying a Leeds man were bright if I could swing it. I didn't see much of a down side."

"And what about the library?"

"Oh I kept going, true to the word according to Frank. And I kept reading and writing. I really was home schooling myself and using the university purely for personal pleasure and social life."

"I definitely want to go into more of that next time but let's round out our time with just a few more wrap-up things if you don't mind? Is that OK?"

She sat up straight again before she answered.

"Sure. I'm starting to like this."

"Great. Alright then, where is your father now?"

"He died from liver disease when I was 20."

"What did you think about that?"

She looked down and away from him and her demeanor changed. "I felt terrible that I didn't cry at his funeral." She stopped talking for a moment and then went on. "I tried very hard to cry, but I simply couldn't." She stopped again and swallowed hard. "He slowly and selfishly killed himself, never properly providing for me or my mum or my sisters." Tears were welling up in her eyes. "He left us nothing when he died, nothing but bills."

"How did your mother take it?"

"I don't know. I remember telling her the night of his funeral that he at least could've loved us. I remember saying to her that at least he could've done that." She sniffled quietly. "She never looked at me when I said those things. She just kept looking out the window. I haven't spoken with my mother or my sisters since that day."

"What did you do to take care of yourself?"

"I left Leeds and came here to London."

"How did that go?"

"When I got here I had no prospects for employment. I had almost no money. The only thing I had was a new beginning. I mean I had my education, Zappa style, but that doesn't come with a degree. I had no particular skill sets. So I looked for a job waiting on tables."

"Where were you living?"

"At first I was in a cheap flop house near the Dickens museum. I used almost everything I had to put the down payment on a month's rent. I spent the first two weeks going to interview after interview, but my lack of experience was killing me. I was getting desperate and really short on money. I got an interview for a waitress position at a small restaurant called Las Iguanas. I walked into the manager's office in the back room and sat down to wait for him. The guy asks me all the questions I expect, but this time I'm ready. When he asks me whether I've waitressed before I pull out a card and give it to him. As he reads it I tell him that I've worked in places in Leeds. This was a lie. I tell him that I was out of work because I wanted to move to London for a life in the big city. That was a lie too. When he asks me where I worked in Leeds I refer him to the card I'd handed him. He says he's never heard of the place. I tell him to call the number on the card and he would reach the manager; that she was expecting calls for references. He lifts the phone off of the receiver and dials. He has a shit eating grin like he's expecting to catch me in the lie. He says, "Hello, may I speak with Beth George please." There is a pause. I hear him say, "Ms. George, this is the manager of Las Iguanas in London. I'm interviewing Edith Hatcher for a position waiting on tables. She tells me she's worked for you. What can you tell me about her?" There is a long pause and I hear him again, "Well, that's sure helpful Ms. George. Thank you. I think that's all I need to know."

"What then," says Lunat.

"He puts the phone down and looks at me. He says your old boss sure had good things to say about you. Tell you what, let's give it a try. Come in tomorrow at around 1 to fill out all of the forms and that rubbish and you can start preparing for the dinner shift at 3. I pay 2 pounds an hour and I give you your schedule every Monday for the upcoming week. Does that sound alright? When he finishes I make up some nonsense about having a few other jobs on hold, but I tell him this feels right and that we should give it a go. I tell him I'll see him the next day."

"But you didn't work in Leeds."

"Nope. But I asked my old piano teacher for a favor. I told her how desperate I was and she agreed to play the part of my old boss. I cooked up a fake card and gave it to this guy and she was ready for his call."

"So how did it work out?"

"I worked at Las Iguanas for six months. I worked my ass off and saved everything that I could possibly save. I learned the benefits of deception. I had never really pulled that off before, and it seemed easy and innocent enough."

"What happened after six months?"

"Well, I had six months of steady and real experience, which in the restaurant business is a good solid run. So I started to look for other more lucrative opportunities. I finally found a good job at the restaurant in the casino. The pay was better. I was able to save more. I worked really hard, long hours. To let off some steam I started to play blackjack. I never took more than I could afford to lose. But I didn't lose. I won. I started to play in the poker room and I won there too. Believe it or not, I quit my job and now I play poker for a living. "

Lunat sat back and folded his arms. He looked at his watch.

"This all has been very interesting and I have a ton of notes to look over. But I'm afraid our time is up, a bit past actually. You'll come back, won't you?"

"I will," she said. "Let's set my next appointment."

Lunat looked at his appointment book. "Same time Thursday next?"

"Thursday next it is. Thank you. I don't know why, but I've actually enjoyed it."

Lunat watched her leave through the door from the waiting room. He also saw his next patient, waiting for his appointment which was already past due.

But he was too intrigued not to look right away at one of the things that Edith had referred to. He closed the door to his office and sat down at his computer. He searched for the poetry of Emily Dickinson until he found the poem that had touched Edith so. He read it from the screen, which glowed in the darkness of his office:

"A Door just opened on a street –

I, lost, was passing by,

An instant's width of warmth disclosed,

And wealth and company.

The Door as sudden shut, and I,

I, lost, was passing by,

Lost doubly, but by contrast, most,

Enlightening misery."

Lunat read it again.

Chapter 15

Edith left the therapist's office in good spirits. She bounded down the street, walking swiftly and pumping her arms with each full stride. She felt lighter.

She heard her stomach growl. She was hungry. She was not very familiar with this part of town so she did not know right off where she could go to get a quick, inexpensive bite to eat.

She decided to venture off of the beaten path and took a right turn on a narrow cobble stone street that headed in the direction of the river. She hoped to find a small neighborhood pub or sandwich shop with a nice view and maybe a table outside.

A man approached her on the narrow sidewalk and tipped his cap and said cheerfully "Good day miss." She nodded back and smiled as he passed and she thought to herself, "A very good day indeed." She crossed the street and peered down the alley for signs of a place to eat. She spotted a wooden sign down about two blocks and although she could not read it from this distance she thought it looked enough like the crest of a pub that she headed toward it. As she approached and the sign became readable she saw that it was indeed the Shepherd's

Place, a pub which almost surely had a lunch menu. She walked quicker toward it and her stomach grumbled again. She took a quick glance around to see whether anyone was close enough to hear.

She stepped through the door and out of the sun and into what seemed, at least until her eyes adjusted, to be almost total darkness. When things came back into focus and she was oriented again to the light, she saw a small crowd of people at tables sipping pints and looking at menus. She glanced over to the bar and saw a few people spread out among the stools, and an amiable looking bartender cleaning mugs and glasses.

"Hello, mate," she said cheerfully to the man behind the bar.

"Good afternoon, miss," he said, smiling back at her and waving his hand towel in her direction.

"Would you like a table or a booth or would you prefer to sit at the bar?"

She thought for a moment. "I think I'll just sit up here at the bar."

"Alright, then, what can I get for you this after?"

"A pint of Betty's Blonde and a menu please."

"Of course, miss. Here's your menu and I'll fetch your pint right away. The special's not on the menu. Bangers and mash with apple cider gravy, three pounds and a half."

By the time he was finished speaking she had her beer in front of her.

"Thank you," she said as she grabbed the pint glass and lifted it to her mouth. She took a small sip and savored it. She ran her eyes over the menu and they stopped decisively on the Dreadnaught, a giant fish sandwich served with fresh homemade chips. She slapped the menu closed and waited for the barkeep to come back around to her side of the bar.

"Decided have we?"

"I have. I'll take the Dreadnaught and a little hot sauce on the side."

"I'll put that order right in miss. Doing ok with your pint?"

"Good for now. Thanks."

Edith sipped her beer and watched the midday news on the television, glowing above the rows of whiskey and other liquors. It was World Cup football time and all of England was excited for her boys on the pitch. The newscaster was happily reporting that England had, as expected, made it out of its group into the final round of sixteen, the knockout round. England would face Germany in the next match. Emotions and national pride would be running high in both countries for the next days leading up to the match. Edith smiled as she thought how silly grown men are when it comes to football. Then she thought about her talk with Lunat and her early infatuation with the game. She smiled.

She was watching the weather report when her sandwich arrived.

"Here you go miss. Can I get you anything else at the moment? Shall I refresh the pint?"

"That would be good, thank you. And I'll need an extra napkin please. This sandwich is a monster."

"It is a big one, isn't it? Rare that anyone finishes it really. Enjoy."

He went to get her another pint and she dug into the battered fish and the nicely fried chips. It felt good to eat real hot food. When she was playing cards she often munched on wafers or candy bars to keep her energy up and more often than not was too tired to cook a proper meal when she got home from a long stretch at the tables. Good beer, good fish, good chips; her day was just getting better by the minute.

Edith looked at her watch and was very surprised to see that it was almost 2 o'clock. She asked for her bill and paid it with small bills and change she counted carefully from her purse. She placed the money on the bar and got up to use the bathroom before heading out for the bus. She peed and then she looked in the mirror to make sure she looked proper. She refreshed her lipstick and licked her finger and ran the wet tip under her eyes to wash away a little run of mascara here and there. She fixed her hair and headed back out into the pub.

"Bye, miss," the bartender called to her as she headed for the door. "Come see us again."

"Will do," she said back at him. "Thanks."

"Our pleasure," he said, as she walked out the door and back into the sunlit street.

She stopped a moment to get her bearings. Coming out of the bar was a bigger shock to her eyes than going in had been. Once she acclimated herself to the light and the location she decided on a direction which would most likely get her to the bus stop. She was full and a little buzzed from the two pints and in a light hearted mood. As she walked it struck her suddenly that she did not miss, in fact had not even thought of, her husband. But today even this did not foul her mood.

As she walked back up the street she decided it was too nice a day to head straight back to her flat so she veered off and toward the river. As soon as she turned the corner she felt the cool breeze; it felt wet and she thought she could taste the cool water on her tongue. She started to smell the river, the water, the boats, and the fish, everything sensual. She felt the sun on her face and the wind in her hair and she realized she was smiling a big smile.

She was swinging her purse back and forth as she walked. She crossed the street and entered the small park that was built along the banks of the river. To her left was a small playground with mothers and children running and laughing and playing and living. The children were loud and very high pitched. The mothers gathered in small discrete groups and gossiped about neighbors, husbands, bosses, churches, and whatever came to mind on this lovely Thursday afternoon in the middle of London.

Edith found a bench facing the water and toward the west and the afternoon sun. She folded her arms on her chest, clutching her purse to her breast and closed her eyes. She was nearly asleep when she felt the weight of someone else on the wooden slats underneath her. She opened her eyes and saw a middle aged woman with a plastic bottle of water who had just taken a seat on the other end of her bench.

"Sorry if I disturbed you. I hope you were not napping."

"Oh no," Edith said. "I was just resting my eyes and daydreaming."

"Certainly a fine day for that, it is," the lady said. "It is a fine day indeed."

"Quite," said Edith.

The lady twisted the cap off of the water bottle and took a sip. "Oh my, that is good. I get so thirsty on these sunny days. I get so very thirsty."

Edith had no response so she stayed quiet.

"Do you live in roundabouts here?" the lady asked.

"No, ma'am. I had a meeting here this morning and thought I would stop here by the park before taking the bus back home. You?"

"Yes. That's why I asked really. I come here most days about this time, weather permitting of course, to pass a half hour or so by the river, in the sun, listening to the little darlings laugh and play. I find it really gives me a boost. It really does. Odd, isn't it?"

"Oh no, I don't think it's odd at all ma'am. I think you have a great ritual, I do. Most people never stop long enough in the day to make any of it worthwhile. I think you've got a great little ritual indeed."

"Well, I think maybe you're right. Anyway, I keep doing it and it works for me."

They sat without talking for a few minutes. Edith heard the woman sigh. Off in the distance the children played and ran and jumped, and you could hear their laughter and yelping and calling to one another.

"Do you have children?" the woman asked Edith.

"No, my husband and I don't."

"Pity," she said.

The lady closed her eyes and hummed a tune very faintly and she smiled. After a few minutes she opened her eyes and sat straight up.

"Well, my time is up for today. Nice talking with you," she said to Edith as she stood up and walked off.

"Nice talking with you ma'am," Edith said, and the lady waved goodbye.

Edith glanced down at her watch. It was a few minutes before 3 o'clock in London. She took a final full breath of the fresh river air. She got up to start walking back to the bus stop. She heard her cell phone ringing from inside her purse. She fumbled around quickly to find the phone and pulled it out after about four rings. She looked at the caller id and saw that it was her husband. Knowing that the call would soon go to her voicemail, she pushed the button to answer as quickly as she could. She wasn't in the mood to talk but she thought she owed him at least the courtesy of a live answer.

"Hello, love. Let me call you…"

She was interrupted by a loud and urgent voice, "No, Edith, no. Don't hang up. Do not hang up."

His tone was alarming and it was plenty enough to get her full attention.

"OK, love. OK. What is it?" She stopped walking and cupped a hand over the earpiece so she could hear.

He calmed down a bit, realizing now that she would not hang up abruptly as usual with a meaningless promise to call right back.

"Listen to me Edith. This is very important. Something has gone bad wrong. I don't have a lot of time for this call and I have been struggling all morning with how to tell you this over the phone a half a world away and with a time limit for the discussion."

"Just tell me, man. Just tell me. What happened?"

"Oh god help me Edith. God help me."

"You, asking for god's help? You're scaring me now. Tell me what happened."

The Brit blurted it out, "I killed a man last night."

The world stopped for Edith. The boats on the river stood still. The children in the park were quiet. The mothers in their groups stopped talking and they seemed to be looking right at her. The sun grew cold. There was no breeze. She slowly sat back down on the bench. All the while a voice was spewing from the phone, but she did not hear, could not listen.

"Edith, are you alright? Edith say something please sweetie say something so I know you're alright. Honey, are you there? Edith, please talk to me. I'm scared to death."

She finally managed to speak. Her voice shook. "You killed a man? Are you fucking kidding because this is a very bad joke, a very bad joke indeed and I'm not laughing love. You don't hear laughing do you?" She paused to catch her breath. "You killed a man? Are you crazy?"

The Brit cut her off, "Edith please, you have to listen to me. I didn't mean to. It was a horrible mistake. It just happened. I wanted my money back. I was winning big love, big enough to make it all right for us again. I was winning bigger than I've won in such a long, long time. Everything was good, love, until this guy shows up and with a few unbelievably lucky hands he takes it all away from us love. He takes it all away. I couldn't let him. I couldn't let him take all of that from us without him giving me at least a chance for getting it back. I fucked up love. Oh god I fucked up. But I couldn't resist the urge to go after that money. I couldn't resist the urge to get the money back so I could feed the urge to keep playing that fucking card game. Oh love, what am I going to do? Do you understand love? I thought you would be the one person who could understand. Oh please tell me you at least understand that I couldn't resist the impulse to get that money back and to keep playing poker. What am I going to do?"

There was a long silence broken only by heavy breathing and sobbing from the Brit.

"I don't know," she finally said. "How could I possibly know?"

"Edith, I am in a county jail in Nevada. I don't even know what happens next? I met a lawyer a few nights ago and I left her a voice message but I haven't heard back from her yet. If she doesn't call soon I'm not sure what I can do. Oh love I'm so fucked."

Again, she made no reply.

"Edith?" he said, softly.

Her mind was spinning uncontrollably. Finally, she answered him with questions of her own, "How did it happen? How did you get caught? How long have you been in jail?"

She started to realize how much she didn't know or understand.

"Love, there are a million questions that you need to ask and that I need to answer, but I have no time now. They could come at any second and tell me my time is up. So please listen. I don't know where we get the money but you need to come here right away. I am all alone here love, all alone and worlds away from home. I need you to be here so we can figure out what we do. Please, love, tell me before they make me hang up that you'll be here."

"My head is throbbing. I can't think straight. How do I get in touch with you?"

"You don't, unless you come to visit me. I can't get phone calls, I can make one or two a day."

The Brit could hear footsteps in the hallway.

"Love they are coming to tell me to hang up. Please tell me you will…"

She heard a low masculine voice in the background.

"Your time is up," and she could hear her husband muttering something in response and then, "OK. A little longer but you need to wrap it up. You got it?"

She heard her husband say, "Alright, just ten seconds."

"Love, I have to go. Please come. I need you."

She floundered for just a second and she heard the man again.

"OK, that's it." And the phone went dead.

The Brit laid his head down on the table in front of him and started to cry.

Edith could barely breathe. Her heart was racing. She felt tightness from the back of her neck to the middle of her chest. She was nauseated. She started to feel her teeth floating in her mouth. She knew she was going to throw up. She stood up and, all the while bent over, she ran to the river. She hung her head over the railing and brought her lunch up and it fell down from her mouth and floated away on the surface of the river. Within minutes, sea gulls were perched on the water eating her vomit. This made her sick again, and she repeated.

Chapter 16

It was 5:25 a.m. on Thursday in Las Vegas, five minutes before the alarm was set to go off. Del squinted at the clock, half awake, and felt for the switch to turn it off. There was no need to wake his wife. She looked so peaceful. He turned and dropped his legs over the side of the bed as softly as he could to keep from disturbing her. His feet felt the floor and he put his weight down lightly and eased out of the bed. He gathered his balance and waited for a second to feel comfortable with his first steps of the day.

He extended his right arm and felt his way around the corner and toward the bathroom. He slid his hand across the exterior wall of the walk-in closet to maintain his course and felt for the end of the wall. He slipped his right hand around the corner and pressed the light switch. The starter for the halogen lights hummed in the silence. He turned on the individual light above his sink, and stopped. He strained to hear if his wife or the dog, sleeping on the floor next to the bed, had heard him. Hearing nothing, he reached for the toothbrush and pulled it from the pewter holder. He brushed quietly, he rinsed and he spat quietly, and he finished.

The bath towels were hanging over the ends of the deep tub that sat in the middle of the large master bath. He grabbed the one closest to him and pulled it around his waist. He did not like to be naked even when he was alone. He shook the shaving cream. He turned on the hot water and as it heated he poured lather into his hand. He looked past himself at the images in the mirror and saw palm trees swaying in the early morning breeze, lit only by the moon. Pulling the razor across his face against the grain, he shaved. He did not rinse the excess lather from his face. He dropped the towel over the side of the tub and got into the shower. Stepping back, he turned on the hot water and waited. When it was hot, he got under the shower head and looked straight up into the stream and let it pour down.

"God it's early and I'm tired," he thought. "I won't be home until late tonight. I have another new case. A murder case. I'm already looking forward to going back to bed. A good long restful sleep is what I need. Tonight, for sure, yes tonight."

He washed his body and he washed his hair. He did not linger. He turned on the other shower head that he could use to rinse the soap from the shower window and the floor. He cleared the soap and turned it off.

Stepping onto the mat outside the shower door, he grabbed the towel and dried off. He felt his face to see whether he had missed any spots while shaving and he was satisfied he had not. "Coffee would be good right now," he thought. He felt his face one more time, and looked in the mirror to see if his nose hairs needed to be trimmed.

He put the towel around his waist and walked into the dressing area. He let the towel drop from his waist and pulled on the under shorts he had laid out the night before. He pulled on the black socks left right beside the shorts, and pulled a white tee shirt over his head. He looked at the closet and picked out a grey suit. He took the pants off of the hanger and pulled them on. He looked for a dress shirt, and chose blue. The collar was tight. He hated wearing suits.

The ties were arranged individually in small wooden squares in a pull out drawer and he chose an Italian silk with dark blue and red stripes. He used one of the full length mirrors in the dressing room to tie the knot. He got his shoes and held them in his hand. God they're nice shoes, he thought.

Good – there was still no stirring from the bedroom. So far he had managed to not wake any one.

He went back to the bathroom and turned out the light. It was very dark again. Carrying his shoes, he walked quietly to the staircase and went downstairs slowly.

"It would be nice to say goodbye and give her a kiss, but I'm sure she'd rather sleep at this hour," he thought.

He left the coffee on the granite island in the kitchen and went back to get his briefcase. He grabbed the case and grabbed the coffee and grabbed his suit coat and turned out the light and went into the attached garage. The garage door whined and squealed and creaked and clawed and screeched and finally opened. He put the coffee into the cup holder and started the car. He backed out into the driveway and closed the garage door.

He always watched to make sure the door closed for safety, and when he saw it was closing he turned the car around and headed down the driveway.

As he merged onto the interstate, he thought how odd it was that so many people were up and about at this hour. The radio played. Where was everyone going? What was on their minds? What are they worrying about today?

"You have to be thinking of something," he thought. And then his mind went blank.

It was 6:45 a.m. when he pulled the parking ticket out of the machine at the parking lot in front of the district attorneys' offices. It was 6:57 a.m. when he passed through security. It was 6:58 when he tied his nice shoes for the second time. It was 7:05 a.m. when he got to his desk.

As expected there was a manila folder on his desk. He sat down and opened the folder. There was not a lot in it. There were reports from the night before describing in detail what the police had found at the scene, what the witnesses had said, what the hotel security knew, etc. There was a description of the manner and cause of death, and there was an affidavit for a search warrant of the Brit's hotel room. But bottom line, Del thought after reviewing what was there, this is a slam dunk conviction. The guy was caught red handed minutes after clubbing the other guy in the head with a lamp. Sometimes, he thought, there should be a simpler way to get from A to Z. This doesn't even deserve a trial.

As he poured himself a cup of coffee in the break room he thought this one was an easy one to add to the old win column. The win column is very important to a DA with political or career aspirations. He would take it, he thought, and he went back to his desk to call his boss.

"Hey boss, Del here."

"Hey Del, how are you this morning?"

"I'm just fine. I got the new homicide you assigned to me. Am I missing something or is this open and shut?"

"O and S, my man. O and S. This British guy freaked out or something after losing a shitload in the poker room. In the midst of his freak out he apparently chases the guy who won upstairs and ends up clobbering him with the fucking lamp. The guy makes it through surgery but dies a few hours later in the ICU from a blood clot or something. The victim manages to dial hotel security who listens in on the whole fucking thing. You have an audio tape of the whole fight and the hotel dicks get to the hotel room seconds after the English guy goes lights out on the other guy."

"Is he lawyered up yet?"

"Don't think so. He was a little drunk and confused so I'm sure we'll know more by the end of the day."

"OK. I'm on it. Once we see who is representing him do we want to talk deal?"

"Let's talk about that after we see who he gets. Just keep me posted, but I'm not too worried on this one. Unless I hear from you I'm going to assume we are on the fast track to an easy conviction or plea. OK?"

"You got it."

Chapter 17

Mary Roys got to her office at around 8:00 on Thursday morning. She was expecting an ordinary day and had a light schedule: a call at 10:00 and a lunch appointment at 12:30. She planned to spend the rest of the day catching up on emails and reading deposition transcripts that had been piling up for weeks.

"Hi, Phyllis," she said to the receptionist.

"Good morning, Mary," Phyllis said, without looking up from the morning newspaper. Phyllis was straining over the crossword puzzle and tapped her pen gently against her right temple.

Mary walked down the hall and opened the door to her office. She took off her jacket and hung it on the hanger on the coat rack to the left of the door. Mary stopped for a second to look out over the city below. Las Vegas did not wake up like other cities. Even though the sun was shining brightly the city seemed asleep.

Mary had a little headache from the wine and after dinner drinks the night before. She pulled a bottle of water from her large purse and opened her desk drawer to look for the Tylenol. She took three with a large gulp of water and pressed her hands against her temples and massaged away some of the pain. "I'll feel better soon," she thought to herself and she sat down in the leather chair behind her desk.

There was a pile of mail in the inbox and a pile of pink phone message slips left by her secretary. The message light was blinking on the phone and the computer screen said she had new mail. She pulled the computer keyboard tray from underneath the desk and began to type in her password. She checked new messages quickly, deleting the obvious junk and filing the less urgent in her "To Read" file. She glanced quickly over the ones that seemed the most important. After about fifteen minutes she concluded that there were no messages that required immediate attention so she pushed the tray back under the desk and swiveled the chair around so she could face the phone.

Mary hit the speaker button and then hit the play new messages button. She grabbed a notepad so she could write down anything important.

"You have 13 new messages," the voice assistant said, continuing with, "playing new messages."

"Hey, Mary, it's Tom Phillips here. It's about 4:30 on Wednesday. Listen, I am really jammed up and I need to put off the Davis deposition. I'm really sorry for the late notice but the shit has really hit the fan here and I need a favor. Let me know right away if we can work that out. Thanks, Mary. Call me soon."

She scribbled to call Phillips about Davis and listened to the next message.

"Ms. Roys I got your name from Bob Short in Chicago. As you know, Mr. Short is with Gilkerson and Shaw. I am with an attorney rating agency in London and we are reviewing Mr. Short's performance for our next publication. He listed you as a reference. If you are willing to…."

Mary hit the erase button and did not write anything down.

"Mary, this is Mike Barnes from Global Chemical. I'm taking over for Mary Warner in litigation and I'm getting the benzene docket. I'll be your new contact and I'm calling to introduce myself and to schedule a time to go over the cases and our strategies forward. Please call me. I look forward to working with you."

Mary tapped her pen on the tablet and knitted her brow. "Mary Warner replaced?" she thought. She made a note to call Mike Barnes ASAP.

Mary listened through several more messages and none were out of the ordinary.

"Ms. Roys," said a voice which she recognized but could not immediately place. The accent was British and the voice was shaky. "I met you the other night in the casino bar, the Prime. I hope you remember. I'm the British bloke who chatted with you for a few minutes. You gave me your card." His voice trailed off and broke as he continued. "I am afraid I need legal help and right away. You see, I got myself in quite a jam earlier tonight and I'm in the county jail charged with murder. I don't have much time to explain now…"

Mary's message machine had a time limit and the Brit had used up his time without giving his number. Mary quickly moved to the next message to see if he had called back. It was him.

"OK, quickly this time because I won't get another call tonight. Please call me at" and she wrote down the number as he gave it.

Mary leaned back as far as she could in her chair and ran her hand across her forehead. "Holy shit," she thought, "murder?"

She got up and paced her way around to the small refrigerator she kept in the bottom of the bookcase, hidden and out of the way. She pulled out a Diet Coke. She opened the can took a sip. She went back to her desk and started to dial.

"Natalie."

"Hey, Mary. What's up? I haven't spoken to you two days in a row in five years. Everything ok?"

"Yeah, everything's fine. But I just got the weirdest call"

"What is it? What's going on?"

"You're gonna need some background. Do you have a few minutes now?"

"Not really," she said with a laugh, "but you've got me so curious I'll make the time. Shoot."

"Are you sure?"

"Yeah, I'm all ears."

"OK. Well, the night before last I gave a talk at the medical causation conference in town. You know the one right?"

"Yeah. I do."

"OK. Well, when I was done I stopped at the bar to have a drink before heading home. I go into the bar and I start talking to a bartender I know there and this British guy starts to hit on me."

"Yeah. Was he cute?"

"Irrelevant. Anyway, so I do my thing to put him off and tell him I don't really like boys, you know the deal, and instead of shying away he gets interested and we chat innocently for a little while until I have to leave. He is actually pretty interesting, despite being a little bizarre. Before I go he asks me for my card and for some reason I give it to him."

"OK."

"So I don't think anything more about it. This morning I get into the office and this guy's left me a message saying he is locked up in County and that he's been charged with murder. He says he needs legal help right away."

"No fucking way. Do you think it's for real?"

"He sure sounded shaken up. I should probably listen to the messages again to see if I can catch any background noise, but I'm telling you I think it's for real."

"What are you going to do?"

"I don't know. I really don't know. I mean I figure the guy used one of his only phone calls to reach out to me so I'm thinking I have to respond. But I can't take the case. Shit I haven't done any criminal law since right out of law school and that was nickel and dime stuff compared to this."

"Well, yeah. This guy's life is at stake and he needs a criminal pro. Do you have anyone in mind?"

Mary paused. "Not really. You know how it is; the civil and the criminal bar might as well be on different planets. Do you know anybody?"

"Not off of the top of my head," Natalie said, "but I'll give it some thought and try to get right back to you."

"Thanks, because I think I need to at least call back this morning."

"OK. Give me about 30 minutes."

"Thanks, talk to you soon."

"Later," Natalie said and hung up.

Mary stood up and walked toward the plate glass window. She stared out in the direction of the city hall, which stood right next to the county courthouse and the county jail. She focused on the jailhouse and imagined what might be happening inside.

Mary and Natalie both got distracted with other things. They did not talk again in 30 minutes or any other time that day.

The Brit was in his small cell. He did not know why but they had put him in his own lockup. Every time he heard footsteps he jumped up to see if a guard was on the way to his space. He was anxiously awaiting one of two calls, one from Mary and one from his wife. So far, every time he jumped up he sat back down disappointed.

He jumped up and saw a guard approaching.

"Is there someone on the phone for me, mate?" he yelled before the guard could even get close to his cell.

The guard stepped in front of his cell and looked in at him. "What'd you say? I know you're new but you can't hear a thing out here until you're right in front of somebody. Jail is lots of things and one for sure is loud. So man if you need to get somebody's attention you got to yell like a son of a bitch. Understand?"

"Sorry, mate," the Brit said. "I was asking if someone was on the phone for me?"

"Oh, ok. No, man. Weren't nobody on the phone for you. They just sent me to see if you were eating anything. Man, you haven't touched your tray."

"How can I eat? I'm scared to death."

"I'm sure bro, but one thing I care about is keeping you alive and healthy while you're with us on my watch so why don't you help me out by eatin' a little something and then tryin' to get some sleep?"

The Brit thought a favor here might be some time returned so in spite of his total lack of appetite he walked over to the corner of the cell and picked up the tray.

"This looks bloody awful," he said and he put a forkful of greasy breakfast potatoes into his mouth. He chewed quickly to get over the bad taste and took a few more bites until the tray was about half empty. He took a sip of the milk from the cardboard container and he put it all back down.

"There you go mate," he said, "I gave her a go."

"Good. You want me to take it away?"

"Please do."

The guard started to walk away and the Brit shouted after him.

"Wait a second please."

The guard stopped and turned back toward him.

The Brit went on, "Can you tell me what happens to me next? I mean I've no idea. I'm not from here. Can you give me just a little help, a little information?" The Brit looked pathetic and the guard felt sorry for him.

"OK, look man," said the guard and his voice got softer and he looked down the corridor to make sure he was not being watched, "I'm not supposed to talk to any inmate here about this shit, and I could get in a lot of trouble. But you seem like an ok dude and I know you're scared. So I'm about to tell you some shit but once I'm done talkin' this conversation never occurred. You understand?"

"Sure, mate, totally. I never heard a word from you."

"Alright then. Now I ain't no lawyer so this could be all wrong but here's how I think it goes down from here."

"OK. No guarantees."

The guard checked down the hallway again before going on, "You've already been booked. That's what they did here when they took all of your information, took your picture, all of that shit. Since you were charged with a heavy crime you got put in the jail. That's where you're at in the process right now. Ok, so here we are."

The Brit nodded.

"The next thing that's going to happen is called the arraignment. But that won't happen until you get a lawyer. You got a lawyer?"

"No, I called the only one I know in Las Vegas, but I haven't heard back from her?"

"How much money do you have?"

"Very little, I'm afraid."

"Then kiss that lawyer's ass good bye. If you can't get a lawyer to do it for free, what they call *pro bono* or some shit like that, you're looking at 100 grand to defend your ass. It sounds to me like you're gonna get in line with the public defender's office. You know, where the court appoints you a lawyer that's paid for by the county or the state, or somebody but not you."

"Why would they give me a lawyer?"

"Because they have to; you got a right to counsel in this country, dude."

"Are they any good? These free lawyers, I mean."

The guard smiled. "Nobody knows 'cause they're too overworked to pay enough attention to any one case. Your situation ain't good man, it ain't good."

"Shit," the Brit said under his breath.

"Anyway, once you get a lawyer the arraignment will be scheduled and you'll get walked outta here over to the courthouse. They'll read the charges against you and then ask you to enter your plea."

"What are my choices?"

"Look, man. If I'd gone to law school I wouldn't be looking after chumps like you in here." He looked around again to make sure he was not drawing any attention.

"I know," the Brit said, "but anything you can tell me really helps."

"Aw, shit. OK. Well, as far as I know you can plead guilty, or if the judge allows it you can plead some shit called no contest, they have a fancy Latin name for it but I always forget, or you can plead not guilty."

166

The Brit mulled these options over in his head. Guilty sounded real bad and no contest seemed to him to be not much better. "How can I plead not guilty with what they know?" he thought to himself. He caught himself daydreaming and focused back to the conversation.

"I suppose not guilty means you have to prove you did not do it?"

"No, man. You ain't got to prove shit. Here the state has to prove that you did it, not the other way around. Shit, you don't even have to testify if you don't want to."

"Really?" the Brit said, more to himself than to the guard.

"Yeah. You know, you have the right to remain silent like they told you when they arrested you. Don't you remember all that bullshit they read to you when they were bringing you in?"

"That continues on through the trial?"

"As far as I know."

"Interesting."

The guard looked nervously down the hallway and fidgeted back and forth from one foot to the other. "I gotta get back."

"Thanks," said the Brit.

"Thanks for what?"

"Right. My mistake," and he smiled at the guard to thank him.

The guard nodded and turned and walked away.

The Brit sat down on the crude bench in his cell. "Guilty, no contest, not guilty," he kept thinking to himself.

He heard footsteps again and it was a different guard.

"Get up in there," said an unfriendly voice. "They want you up front."

The Brit stood up right away and as he was being handcuffed and pulled from the cell he managed to say "Can you tell me what for?"

"No, I can't," the guard said, with a stern emphasis. "They'll tell you what for. I just get you there."

The Brit stayed quiet. The guard led him down the hall and he heard others in the cells jeering and calling. The guard was taking him toward the room with the telephone and his pulse quickened. He did not know which call to mentally prepare for, the one with his wife or the one with the lawyer that he barely knew. It does not matter, he thought, I don't know what I should say no matter which one is on the phone.

"You have a call in there." The guard put him in the room and locked the door behind him. The Brit put his wrists through a very small opening in the thick door so the guard could undo his handcuffs. When his hands were free he shook his wrists to muster up circulation and turned to pick up the phone. His hands were shaking and his palms were sweating.

"Hello," the Brit said and the tone of his voice indicated the question at the front of his mind. "Who is this?"

"This is Mary Roys," and before the Brit could say anything she was continuing, "I got your voice message this morning and I'm returning your call."

"Oh Ms. Roys thank you ever so much for ringing back. I've been a nervous wreck waiting for you to call. Thank you so very, very much."

"You're welcome but I am afraid that based on what you told me in your message I won't be of much help to you," and as he listened his heart sank in his chest. She continued, "You see, I don't practice criminal law. And based on what you told me you really need a good criminal lawyer."

He tried to speak but she jumped in to interrupt, "Don't say a word for now. I don't wanna know what you're charged with or what your story is. The less I know the better. So be quiet and listen, ok?"

He nodded at the phone and then he realized he needed to provide an audible response, "Yeah, sure," he said softly and without any conviction.

"Here is what legal advice I can give you and then we can talk about who might be able to help you," she said.

"OK, fair enough I suppose, please go on."

"The first thing you have to know is that you do not have to talk to the police without a lawyer. So, do not talk to them without a lawyer. Tell them you want to be cooperative but that you are asserting your right to remain silent until you have a lawyer to advise you. That should cut off any further attempts by the police to talk with you. Make a note of when and what you tell them because if they keep trying to talk with you after you've asked for a lawyer that could be a huge help to you later on;

having proof of what you said and when you said it about your right to remain silent will be very important. Do you understand all of this so far?"

"Yes, yes, I think I do."

"Listen, most Americans are afraid to exercise their right to not talk to the police so I expect it might even be harder for you. Listen to me carefully on this, the police will not think you are guilty because you refuse to talk without a lawyer. Quite to the opposite they'll think you're smart. They'll be pissed and they'll likely act pissed, but believe me they'll be thinking that you're smart. Do you understand that?"

"Yes, yes I do ma'am."

"OK. Now let's talk about who might be able to represent you…"

"Hold on, ma'am before I waste any of your time. I haven't got the money to pay a lawyer. If I had the money to pay a lawyer I wouldn't be in this trouble.
"

There was a pause and he could sense her thinking on the other end. Finally, she broke the silence, "How much do you have?"

"I have nothing here in this country. And my wife has very little to bring. I suspect we have maybe $5,000 US in savings. I have information that suggests that would not be nearly enough."

"I think your information is accurate. Most good criminal defense lawyers would require a retainer at least five times that to start a murder case."

"Do you know anything about *pro bono* work?" he said, using the phrase from the guard.

She was surprised by the question. "Yes, of course. All lawyers know about *pro bono* work," and as she said the words she thought about the fundraiser and the general apathy of the bar toward putting their efforts where their mouths were.

"Could you see any possibility of a lawyer taking this *pro bono?*"

She searched for the most truthful answer that would inflict the least pain. She said, "Probably not. I could do some digging around though if you would like?"

"That would be very much appreciated ma'am. Very much appreciated indeed."

"I'll do that. But let's talk about a Plan B if that doesn't work."

"Ok, ma'am. What might that be?"

"Well, the state will appoint a lawyer for you if you can't afford one. Have they asked whether you need a court appointed lawyer?"

"I don't think so ma'am. It was all sort of confusing through the night but I don't think so."

"Well, when we get off here tell them you need a court appointed attorney. If we can find someone to do the case *pro bono* we can substitute them in later."

"Alright ma'am. I'll do that. Will you call me back after you dig around a bit for another lawyer?"

"Yes. But now I need to…"

The Brit sensed she was ending the call and he cut her off, "Ms. Roys, please. Just a few more questions while I have you. Please?"

"Alright, but I really do need to be going. I have another call at 10."

"Oh, thank you. Hang on please and we will be done by 10." He gathered his thoughts quickly. "I know you don't want to know the particulars and as you wish I shall spare you all of them. But may I indulge you for a few general questions to confirm some information I have received rather informally up to now?"

She was silent. The Brit went on.

"I understand that I'm here under arrest for murder and that the next step, after I get a lawyer I presume, will be" he looked down at his notes, "an arraignment in court where the formal charges will be read to me and I will be called upon to enter a plea. Do I have it right so far, basically?"

"Basically, yes."

"OK, good enough. Now as I further understand it I have three plea options. First, I could plead guilty. Second, I could plead no contest, which you might know by some other Latin name," and she interrupted him.

"Nolo contendere," she said.

"Right. And third I could plead not guilty. Am I right again so far?"

"Right again."

Then after a brief pause she added, "The only thing you're missing is a plea of not guilty by reason of insanity."

"Ma'am?"

"I said the only thing you've left out is the option to plead not guilty by reason of insanity."

After a silence from the Brit, she went on, "I'm not suggesting anything."

"Right," he said softly.

"OK, I'm sorry but I absolutely have to go, but I'll be in touch. Remember what I told you," and she hung up.

The Brit slowly put the receiver back down. He walked to the door and pounded three times so the guard would know to come and fetch him. He heard the footsteps thumping down the hall. Every sound in jail was amplified a hundred times by the vast iron and concrete openness. When the guard arrived he put his wrist through the small hole and submitted to being shackled around the wrists. He withdrew his hands so the guard could open the door and he stepped out into the hallway as the guard took him by the arm.

"I don't want to talk to anyone until I get a lawyer," he said as he stared straight ahead.

"Can you afford a lawyer?"

"No. I need a lawyer appointed for me."

"I'll pass it on."

The Brit got into his cell and wrote down the date and time and what he told the guard. He curled up in the fetal position and went to sleep.

The guard went to his supervisor and relayed the Brit's message.

"He wants to lawyer up? Ok."

The supervisor turned and started typing an email to Del in the DA's office. The first governmental record of the Brit's assertion of his right to remain silent was made.

Chapter 18

Edith opened the door to her flat and closed it behind her. All the while on her way home, she thought about calling someone. She decided not to.

She packed a small duffel bag with clothes enough for several days and stuffed her essential toiletries into a zip-loc storage bag and shoved the plastic bag into the larger faux leather duffel bag. Once the duffel bag was packed she started opening and closing the drawers in her flat looking for loose change, random bills, anything of value. She searched under seat cushions and in pants pockets and everywhere else where a few shillings might be found. She managed to find about 25 pounds in jean pockets and dresser drawers and other sundry places.

"This is Edith," she listened to the person on the other end for a few seconds and then went on, "yes; I'm fine thank you but in a bit of a rush. I need to check the balance on account 99783647. The password is "straight flush." Ah, the PIN. Wait just a sec," and she rooted through her purse to pull out her small planner. "Bear with me a moment," she said as she found the page with all of her personal identification numbers. "OK, here it is – 28336777."

"Can you tell me the name of your first pet, for security purposes of course?"

"Jagger," she said.

"One more please. Can you tell me your favorite color?"

"Blue."

"Thank you for your patience ma'am and now hold one moment, please."

Edith lit a cigarette and puffed on it nervously. The ashes dropped onto the floor.

"Alright, sorry for the delay," said the pleasant lady from the bank. "You have 4,978 pounds available for withdrawal."

Edith wrote the number down on a pad by the bed. "Thank you," she said and she put down the phone.

She checked her purse for her passport and for her debit card. She had them both. She grabbed her bag and went to the bus stop. She got the express to Heathrow airport.

Edith sat down near the back of the bus. She took the aisle seat next to a middle aged woman who appeared to be asleep. Edith was emotionally spent and physically exhausted. She put her arms across her chest and dropped her chin down and tried to nap. She fell asleep. As the bus whirred on she slept more deeply and slipped into a dream:

Edith is in a poorly lit and very bare room. She is lying on her back on a dirty and unkempt cot. There is a single light bulb hanging from above and perching just inches in front of her face. She is unable to move. The light is irritating her. She cannot close her eyes. She struggles with all of her strength to bring the upper eye lid down to meet the lower eye lid, but they are stuck fast. It hurts her to try and close her eyes.

A small drip of water falls from the bottom of the light bulb onto Edith's upper lip. She cannot move her arms to bring her hand to her face to wipe the water away. She feels a large invisible weight on each of her wrists, and no matter how hard she tries, there is no lifting the weights away.

The drip is unsteady, so that from time to time it seems as if it has stopped. But just then, there is another drop on her face. She thinks that it would be much easier if there was some rhythm to the dripping. The unpredictability is intolerable.

Suddenly, Edith is naked and she is cold. There is a draft that is blowing over her but she cannot see any windows or openings to the out of doors. There is no light but for the solitary, dripping bulb. The air is damp.

Edith squirms in the bus seat. She is asleep and continues to dream.

Edith's eyes are burning with the dryness. She remains paralyzed. The sequence of the drippings repeats.

Now the drip is not water; it is blood. The smell of blood, the feel of blood, and the color of blood is falling on her, one drip by one drip, without rhythm, without rhyme, without reason. It runs slowly into her eyes; red brown opaque pools in her eyes. She cannot close her eyes and the blood stagnates, and stinks.

Edith wakes up in her bus seat and rubs her eyes roughly. She looks around and comes slowly back to reality. She looks out the window and the sun is now set. The woman next to her is awake.

"My dear, you were having quite a dream just now," she said, "I almost was compelled to wake you. I thought you would rub your eyes out, I did. Are you alright?"

"Yes, ma'am," said Edith softly. "Thank you for being concerned. I'll be alright."

The woman looked away and out the window at the lights from the cars streaming past in the other direction. Edith looked down at her hands which were red from the rubbing and the clenching.

The woman turned back to her. "Where are you off to tonight, may I ask?"

"New York. And then onto Las Vegas."

"You don't say? Well, that's a much more exciting trip than mine I dare venture."

"Oh, I don't know. Where are you going?"

"I'm off to see my sister in Brussels. Nothing nearly as glamorous as Las Vegas."

Edith sighed audibly. "I envy you that trip, ma'am. I envy you that trip." Oh, how I envy the ordinary, she thought.

The bus pulled in front of the airport terminal and the passengers disembarked row by row from the first to the last. Edith waited patiently until her row was next and she said goodbye to her seat mate and walked to the front of the bus and out of the door.

British Airways flight 208 lifted off from Heathrow on time. Edith was in seat 67C. Her mind was a million miles away. Her eyes were still sore from the rubbing during the dream.

Chapter 19

As flight 208 made its way across the Atlantic, the Brit slept in his cell.

"Wake up in there, you've got a visitor," the guard said as he banged on the heavy metal door. "Come on, get up."

The Brit lifted his head off of the flimsy, dirty pillow and sat up, rubbing his eyes and running his hand through his hair. "Alright, I'm coming," he answered back. "Who's here to see me?"

"You wanted a lawyer. So the generous state of Nevada got you a lawyer."

The Brit perked up. "I'm to meet him now?"

"Yep, right now. And he probably doesn't have a lot of time so if I were you I'd get your sorry ass up and pick up the pace."

"Right," and as he was saying this he stuck his wrists through the opening to receive the handcuffs.

The Brit was led down a hallway he had not been down before and into a room that appeared a bit nicer than any other in the stark jailhouse. As he entered the room he saw a desk and chairs. Seated at the desk was a man in his late 30's or so with a rumpled suit and a well-worn briefcase. His head was down and he was reading from a file folder. He did not look up when the guard introduced him to the Brit.

"Ring me when you're finished counselor," the guard said as he took the cuffs off of the Brit, left and closed the door behind him. The Brit waited for an invitation to sit down.

After what seemed to the Brit to be an hour the lawyer looked up, "Sorry," he said. "I thought you were already sitting. Please sit down. I'm just finishing up with your file. Go on, sit down and make yourself as comfortable as you can. I'll be just another minute or two."

"Take your time, sir. I've suddenly got plenty of that," and the Brit smiled weakly.

The lawyer closed the file folder and looked at the Brit. He took out a yellow legal pad and pulled a pen from his coat pocket. He took off his suit coat and hung it on the metal folding chair next to him. He pushed the button on the top of the pen and put the pen to the paper and without writing said, "Full name please?"

"T. S. Fowler."

"No, I need your full legal name."

"That's it. T. S. Fowler. My parents named me after T. S. Eliot."

"Did they really?" And he paused to reflect on his undergraduate English Literature major. "Did they ever say why?"

"Not that I recall as to why, no. I don't think I ever really knew why. I just know my father loved his poetry, and that of his mentor Ezra Pound."

And the lawyer said without hesitation, "I should have been a pair of ragged claws / Scuttling across the floors of silent seas".

"*J. Alfred Prufrock,*" said the Brit. "Bravo! My father loved that poem."

"You got it," the lawyer said, and he scribbled down the name of his new client.

"Citizenship?"

"British."

"Current occupation?"

"Gambler, I'm a poker player to be exact."

"For a living?" the lawyer asked.

"Yes," the Brit said, "and my wife does the same."

"Married?"

"Yeah."

"What's your wife's name?"

"Edith."

"Does she know about this?"

"Yes, I called her this morning local time. I asked her to come and I haven't heard back so I'm hoping she'll be here or that I'll at least hear from her soon."

"I hope so too, you're going to need the support."

He hesitated as if reminding himself of something and then went on, "I'm so sorry, busy does not excuse ignorance; I should introduce myself. My name is Bob Scotti. I'm an associate in the county public defender's office. I've been appointed by the state to represent you because you said you can't afford private counsel. Are you good with that?"

"Yeah, I'm absolutely fine with that."

"Good. So I read the file. Don't say anything until I finish summarizing. Understand?"

"Yes."

"OK, good. According to the Las Vegas police report and according to interviews with the hotel security you were playing poker with the victim, he won a big pot and took all of your chips, he left the table, you followed him out and up to his room." He stopped and sipped from the water bottle in front of him on the table. He cleared his throat. "You apparently forced or talked your way into his room. The victim made it to the phone in the front bathroom and called security, the phone line was open from that point on and the police have a recording of the sounds in the room. I haven't heard the tape yet. The report says there was a struggle and that hotel security came into the room while you were cleaning off the doorknob and that there was a lamp, which the report says had been wiped, within your reach and that the victim was lying in his own blood on the floor in front of you. You were drunk and not making much sense. You were placed under arrest and read your rights, at least according to the report. We may get back to that. The victim was taken to the hospital and eventually died from the injuries or complications from the surgery, it sort of doesn't matter for now."

He took another drink.

"Can I say anything yet?" the Brit asked.

"Not yet," Bob said, "in a minute."

"You have been in county since the arrest. You've made two calls, one to a lawyer you apparently know here in town and the other to your wife."

Bob loosened his tie and leaned back in his chair. He asked the Brit, "How much did you have to drink before all of this happened?"

The Brit had the look of someone struggling to remember. "I know I had several drinks in the room before I went back to the table. I can't really remember how much I drank at the table. I was pissed though; here in the states I think you'd say shitfaced. I remember that. I was not thinking clearly." The Brit regrouped, "I was not thinking at all."

Bob scribbled on the pad. He looked up at the Brit and said, "Ever any trouble with the law before?"

"No, nothing really."

"Any prior arrests?"

"No."

"Do you understand the American attorney-client privilege?"

"I think so but it would be better to hear it from you."

"I agree. I like that answer. Here's the deal on the privilege because I am going to start asking you the serious stuff. Almost anything you tell me is confidential. The only way I can break that confidence is if you tell me about something you're planning to do in the future that is criminal, but as far as anything to do with what has already been done, that's all covered by the privilege. So you tell me, then only you, me and my legal staff ever know. I can't help you if you lie to me. You don't have to take the stand and testify in this country, so if you tell me that you killed this man the other night I won't put you on the stand. If you tell me something else, like you didn't kill the guy, well then we'll think long and hard about whether to put you on the stand. Does all of this make sense so far?"

"Yeah, I think so. And I swear I'll tell you the truth. I can't afford not to."

"Good." Bob flipped the page on the notepad and started the meat of his interview.

"When did you first see the victim?"

"I played with him in the poker room the night before all of this happened. He seemed nice enough and we actually chatted a bit. The next time I saw him was at the table last night."

"So you didn't know him before you saw him at the table the night before last?"

"No. He was on a business trip of some sort and as far as I know he was working during the day and playing a little poker at night I guess, but I definitely never met him before the day before yesterday."

"OK. Did you have any problems with him while you were playing, any arguments, any fights, anything he did to piss you off or provoke you?"

"No. Other than kicking my ass with a lucky draw and taking all the money I had been winning over the course of several days. Other than that, he was right peachy."

"We'll get to the hand that set you off later; nothing else besides beating you in the game?"

"Well, he did have a few shitty words for me when he won a hand from me some time earlier, I can't remember if it was yesterday or the night before. But it really wasn't anything that I held on to. It really didn't get under my skin. That's poker. Pricks win and pricks lose and pricks will be pricks."

There was a silence before the Brit went on, "I mean, I'm digging here in my mind for information since you seem to think it's important but it didn't get me all fired up or anything. I just thought this one outburst was fairly severe."

"Fine, I appreciate that. I don't want you to spin it. I just want straight unfiltered answers to my questions."

"That's what you're going to get."

"You want something to drink? Water, soda, coffee?"

"No thanks," said the Brit.

"You sure?"

"Yeah, I'm fine but thanks for bothering to ask."

Bob went on, "Did you follow this guy upstairs after he won the big hand?"

The Brit hesitated for just a second. "Yes. I followed him up to his floor."

"What were you thinking when you decided to follow him up to his floor?"

"I wasn't thinking about following him."

Bob looked at him, slammed down his pen and said, "Don't make me pull teeth here. What were you thinking?"

"I was following the money."

There was a short silence while Bob waited for more information. The Brit stayed quiet.

Raising his eyebrows and his pen, Bob said, "You mind explaining that a little, please?"

"I was following the money. He had my money. Money is the raw material for my work. I was following my money."

"What was your plan, I mean what were you following the money for?"

The Brit thought about that for a while. "I don't think I had a plan. I just was thinking that I had to have the money back or I couldn't play poker anymore. I honestly don't think I had a plan. I was just following the money."

"Well, when did you decide to go into this guy's hotel room? When did you start thinking about action, something you were going to do?"

The Brit leaned his head back and scratched at the back of his neck. He looked at the ceiling while he answered, "I don't know. I remember trying to be logical. I remember thinking for a second that I should go back to the lift and head downstairs. I remember thinking that I should act like a rational adult. But I remember the overwhelming desire to get my money back. And that desire superseded all my other thoughts."

"Go on."

"I remember the first normal thought occurred right before it happened. I was actually going to try to salvage the situation by freeing the victim…"

Bob cut him off, "freeing him from what?"

"I had tied a computer cord around his wrists behind his back."

"Why?"

"To keep him under control while I searched the room for my money."

"OK. Go on."

"Well, like I was saying, I thought to myself I can't really get away with this. I mean I'm finally thinking shit, even if I take my money back how am

I going to get away with it and not be in serious trouble. It was all unraveling in my head. I was drunk. I was confused, I was desperate. I was out of my mind." The Brit paused to catch his breath and gather his thoughts. "So I was just about to untie him and explain how crazy the whole thing was when he broke free on his own and clobbered me in the face. It was instinct from there and I picked up the lamp and wacked him. I felt the bone break under the blow and it was really quite disgusting. Before I could even think much more the door flew open and the hotel security was all over me."

"Did you say anything to them?"

"I honestly don't remember much of anything from then until I was here."

"So you don't know what you said to them?"

"I don't know what I said to them, no."

The public defender leaned back and closed his eyes. He opened them and said, "OK. That gives me enough to think about for now."

Bob opened his eyes and leaned forward. He looked directly into the Brit's eyes and said, "Now that I've been assigned to the case the arraignment will be scheduled pretty quickly. When I hear for sure I'll let you know. Then we'll need to talk about a plea. In the meantime I'm going to talk to the DA to find out what he is thinking."

Bob saw the puzzled look on the Brit's face and he explained, "Sorry, the DA, the district attorney, is the state's lawyer who prosecutes the case against you."

Then Bob finished his thought, "We will see what he is thinking. If he's willing to offer any deals, I'll let you know."

As Bob stood to leave the Brit stood too and said, "Whoa, please. What kind of deal? I don't understand."

Bob sat back down. "Sorry. I'm really tired and most of my clients know more about the criminal procedure than me. Ok, here's how it works. The DA might offer you something called a plea bargain. That means he might offer you a charge less than what is in the indictment against you in exchange for your guilty plea to that lesser charge. Usually, if we can cut the deal we can agree on a sentence to recommend to the judge. The judge doesn't have to accept the deal and he doesn't have to agree to the sentence. But usually the judge goes along as long as the DA and defense lawyer agree."

"What lesser charge and how much time?"

"We're way ahead of ourselves here. But just as an example, you're charged at the top of the ticket with an open murder charge."

"The top of the ticket?"

"Yeah, the highest charge. You're also charged with lesser offenses to hedge the DA's bet, but the state's going for the highest one and so far it looks like they could get it here."

"Go on please."

"OK," Bob said. "Let's say the DA says he'll agree to accept a guilty plea to second degree murder or voluntary manslaughter or something less than first degree. Let's say you agree to enter that plea if he agrees to recommend a sentence near the bottom of the guideline range. That's a plea bargain. But we have nothing to discuss seriously until I talk to him about what he might offer."

"Does it make me look weak or scared for you to talk about a plea bargain now?"

"No. It's all standard operating procedure just to test the waters and weigh the options. It forms the basis for a solid risk benefit analysis. I can assure you that it's very standard operating procedure."

"Alright, so when will I hear from you again?"

"When I need more information from you or when I get an arraignment date."

The Brit dropped his head. "Any idea when?"

"You'll hear from me within a few days, within a few days at most."

Bob rang for the guard. Within a few seconds the door was opened. As Bob was heading out he turned and said, "I know you're scared. I know you're overwhelmed. I know."

Bob looked at T. S. and for the first time recognized him, "Just know this, I'll do my best to help you. I like my job and I do it well. Take care."

"You too," the Brit said and with that the public defender was gone on to his next case. "And thank you," the Brit said as Bob disappeared down the hall.

The guard escorted the Brit back to his room. As soon as he got inside he sat on the bench and tried to recreate the interview with the lawyer, his lawyer, his lawyer in a murder case.

His head ached and so he thought it was better to not think about the interview right now. Instead, he lay back on the bench and closed his eyes and thought about Edith: Edith Fowler, his wife.

He thought about things that she thought. He thought back to the time when he and his wife had real conversations. How they used to talk about important things, things about life and living. A time when they cared about those things, not just about gambling and money. He remembered the verses from Eliot's *The Waste Land* that he always thought of when he thought of her, and he tried to remember why in all of their conversations about literature and poetry and the arts he had always decided not to mention the verses to her. All alone in his cell, with the noises of the cell block ringing and clanging and reverberating in his ears, he still knew the verses by heart. He said them out loud to no one in particular:

"Who is the third who walks always beside you?

When I count, there are only you and I together

But when I look ahead up the white road

There is always another one walking beside you

Gliding wrapt in a brown mantle, hooded

I do not know whether a man or a woman

—But who is that on the other side of you?"

The Brit felt better having said the words. Who was walking by Edith's side? Who was the third wheel? How had they come to be so apart? He was very alone – in every sense of the word.

He felt uncertain of his identity. He was at a loss to express his feelings, even though they were his own. Just like his old friend Prufrock, he thought.

As it got closer to lights out T. S. said "Please be on your way Edith. Please be on your way." He tried to think about the last time they had made love; he still could not remember.

Chapter 20

Edith's flight touched down at JFK just a little behind time. The huge plane strained to stop and eventually lurched into a turn off the main runway. Edith raised the window shade and looked out for the first time on US ground.

Edith had not checked any bags. Her duffel was in the large overhead above her seat. When the plane stopped at the gate and the signal was given Edith stood up and took her bag out of the overhead compartment.

She followed the other passengers into the airport terminal. The line for checking foreign passports was very long. She had plenty of time so it did not matter.

She passed through immigration without any trouble and went to the customs line marked "Nothing to Declare." Since she did not have to wait for baggage she was one of the first in line and moved quickly to the front.

"Here on vacation or business?" the agent said with the normal accusatory tone and stare.

"Neither," she said without thinking.

"What's the purpose of your visit then?"

She hesitated only for a moment. "I'm sorry, it's business. I have to take a meeting in Las Vegas. I'm just very tired after the long flight." She made a feeble attempt at a smile.

"How long are you staying?"

She hesitated again since she hadn't thought about any of this. "It depends on how my meeting goes but I think only a few days."

"Where are you staying in Las Vegas?"

Again, a difficult question to answer. "I had to leave on the spur of the moment, an emergency meeting you might say. I don't know where I'm staying," and thinking quickly she added, "but my assistant is getting me a suite at a suitable hotel and as soon as I'm able to use the phone she'll have my accommodations for me."

He started to ask another question and then he stopped. He was listening to someone talk at him through his earpiece.

"Wait here one moment please" the agent said.

"Shit," she whispered.

She could see the agent go into a room with a large window and pick up a phone. He was talking and then he was listening and then he talked again. He hung up the phone and came back to the line.

"You can go on ahead," he said.

"Thank you," she said and she hurried through, wiping a bit of sweat from her upper lip.

She pulled the duffel bag behind her and made her way through the hallways to the shuttle and to the domestic terminal from which her flight to Las Vegas would depart. She was hungry, tired and very confused.

She found an open seat at the crowded bar near her gate. She put her bag on the floor next to her stool and she wrapped one calf around it to keep it secure.

"Hello," the bartender said. "You need a menu?"

"Yes, please," she said, "and a Bass Ale."

He flipped the menu down in front of her. She looked at the left side and then at the right. She was taken aback by the prices and not knowing how long she would be in the US or how she would find a reasonably priced place to stay, she chose based solely on price. She wished she had seen the menu before ordering the beer and now nursed it since she would only be able to feel comfortable paying for one. It was just as well that she did not choose anything too expensive because when the food came she ate it but did not taste it. All of her senses seemed to be asleep, numb still from the shocking news from the Brit.

She paid her check and glanced down at her watch. She gathered her things and went to the gate. The gate agent said the plane was on time and she found a seat in the waiting area and slumped into it. She stared at the television monitor hanging from the ceiling and watched the news broadcast by CNN.

Her mind wandered and the sounds around her slowly muted and she was in silence. "This cannot be happening," she thought. The ring of her cell phone snapped her out of the daze.

"Hello," she said, not having any idea who was calling because her caller id would not work here in the States.

"Edith, I am so happy you picked up," it was her husband. "Where are you?"

"Are you alright?" she asked, with genuine concern in her voice and she wondered where it had come from.

"Yes, I'm ok, as good as one could expect I guess, but where are you? Can you come? I need for you to come."

"Relax, love. I'm coming. I just landed in New York and I'm waiting for my flight to Las Vegas. I'm on my way."

She could hear him sobbing. She suddenly felt very sorry for him, very sorry for herself, and a feeling for him she had not felt in quite some time. She tried to comfort him, "It's going to be ok, love. It will have to be OK."

He pulled himself together. "I'm just so happy you're on your way. I have no one to talk to. I have no one who cares. I have no one."

"You have me, love. And I'll be there soon." She paused and when she didn't get a quick response she went on, "Can you talk now or are there people listening?"

"There's no one here at the moment but I'm afraid about them listening in. I don't know how it works. So I think it best we keep things rather generic for now. I'll feel much more comfortable when you're sitting across from me."

"I suppose you're right, but it's very hard for me to be so in the dark about what happened, how it happened, why it happened."

"I know. I know. I was there. I am here. And I have the same questions." He sobbed quietly again and she sensed he was trying to keep it from her. "I'm so sorry to be putting you through this. I'm quite an ass."

She paused and, with a bit of a laugh meant to cheer him up a little bit, said, "Yes, dear, quite an ass indeed."

A voice came over the loud speaker that interrupted and preempted their conversation, "In just a moment we will begin boarding Flight 687 to Las Vegas. We will begin our boarding with people needing special assistance and then we will move to the first class cabin…"

The message seemed to go on forever and Edith and the Brit had to wait for it to finish. Finally, there was space to talk.

"Well, as I'm sure you just heard we'll be boarding soon."

The Brit answered, "Yes, and I'm so anxious to see you."

"There is a bit of a knotty problem," she said.

"I'll say," said the Brit.

"No, I mean with my trip. I have no place to stay in Las Vegas."

She could tell he was thinking.

"I've been so consumed with everything here I didn't even think about that. Hotels here are generally quite pricey." She could sense that he was thinking again.

The loudspeaker interrupted again, "Boarding all zones all rows for Flight 687."

"Love, I should go. The flight is overbooked and I don't want to lose my seat."

"Yes, by all means please get on the plane. And have a very good, safe flight. I love you."

She stopped in her tracks. He had not said that in a very long time, so long ago in fact that she could not remember how long. Her mouth was open and she was temporarily at a loss for words.

"I love you too," she said. She closed the flip phone slowly.

T.S., the Brit, cradled the phone against his neck

and cried quietly. He sat for some time. "She is on her way," he thought, and he smiled ever so slightly, redirecting a tear to the corner of his mouth.

When he felt composed he called back to the guard.

"Can I make one more quick call?" he said.

"I shouldn't…"

The Brit cut him off. "Less than thirty seconds, I promise, mate."

"OK. Hurry up."

The Brit hurried to dial Mary Roys. He knew he would get an answering machine and while he heard the ringing he was drafting the message in his head.

"Ms. Roys, this is T.S. Fowler. I have very little time so I must be brief. My wife is on her way here from England and she has nowhere to stay. I can't think of anyone else to ask so could you please call her and help her find a place. I know I have no right to impose and I've already asked too much of you, but please, this one last favor. Her name is Edith and her number is," and he left her Edith's number and ended the message with, "thank you again. You're a saint and I know you'll help. I'm eternally obliged."

He went over his message in his head and wondered if he had been able to elicit enough sympathy to get Mary Roys to go above and beyond the call of duty. He gave himself better than even odds.

He called the guard, "Thanks, mate. That was very kind of you."

He was escorted back to his cell.

Mary Roys was in her car heading home and decided to check office messages. She figured she could bill some time while she sat in the Strip traffic. She got to the message from the Brit.

She listened to it twice and then hit the button to save the message. She didn't know what to think.

The first thing she did when she got home was go to the refrigerator. She poured herself a glass of Sauvignon Blanc. Then she kicked off her shoes, sat on the couch and reached for the phone. She dialed Natalie.

"Hello."

"Hey, Natalie," Mary said, "it's Mary Roys again.

You got a minute?"

"Yeah, sure," she said. "I'm just sitting here proofreading documents. What's up?"

"Well, the weirdest thing."

Natalie curled her legs underneath her butt and sat back on the couch, "Yeah, so let's hear it."

"OK. The British guy called again."

"Are you fucking serious?"

"Yeah, on my way home tonight I'm listening to my messages and he left me another one. He's frantic and rushed and tells me he needs one last favor."

"What favor?"

"His wife's on her way from London and has nowhere to stay. He asked if I could help her find a place."

"You've got to be kidding. What does he think you are a fucking travel agent?"

"I know, I know." She gathered her thoughts and Natalie waited. "But I have the weirdest urge to help. I mean we go to the *pro bono* dinner and we rag on people for not doing any volunteer work and then we talk about our old idealism and then we rag on ourselves for being where we are now and then a guy who is in serious shit, half way around the world from home, calls for some legal help he desperately needs and what do I do? I blow him off. Worse than that, I promise him something I don't even do. I mean how far have I fucking come from wanting to do the right thing? When did my fucking life go off the rails?"

When Natalie did not respond, Mary went on, "And she went to bat to protect her gay friend for no reason other than she thought it was right. I feel like I owe her for that."

Again, Natalie did not answer right away. Finally she said, "Alright. So what're you going to do?"

"That's why I'm calling you again – for a reality check. I have no fucking idea what I'm going to do. I know what I should do."

There was another break in the conversation.

Mary continued, "I'm sitting here drinking and thinking about inviting this stranger to stay here with me."

"Are you fucking crazy?"

"I don't know, am I?"

"You can't do that. This woman's husband is charged with murder. You don't know her or him. I am absolutely telling you this is the craziest fucking thing I have ever heard you say."

Mary took a sip of the wine. "What if I at least call her and offer to pick her up at the airport? I could see how it goes from there."

"I wouldn't return the call and I would forget any of it ever happened."

"Normally so would I," and she took another sip and shook her head to herself. "Normally so would I."

"When does she get here?"

"I don't know. I have her phone number and all he said was she was on her way. I have no idea."

Natalie sounded very serious, "OK. You need to go to bed and forget all about this crazy shit. OK?"

"OK," Mary said, "I know I need to go to bed but there's no way I can forget about this. Hey, thanks for listening. I'll be alright. Good night."

"Good night, but for Christ's sake call me in the

morning."

They hung up.

Mary closed her eyes and sighed, and then she dialed. The call went straight to voice mail.

"Edith, my name is Mary Roys. I live in Las Vegas. Your husband told me you're on your way here and asked me to help you find a place to stay. I'm going to give you my cell number and I want you to call me when you land. OK, here it is….," and she hung up and filled her glass.

She picked up the remote and switched on MSNBC. She watched the program but her mind was going a mile a minute in other directions.

The TV was on and Mary was asleep on the couch when the phone rang and woke her.

"Hello," she said in a sleepy and soft voice.

There was no immediate response and Mary spoke again, "Hello?"

"Hello, ma'am. This is quite awkward. This is Edith Fowler and I just landed in Las Vegas and listened to your message. I finally found the courage to call you and, well, here I am, not really sure what happens next."

Mary tried to wake up and gather herself. "Edith, hello. I'm glad you called and that you got here safely." She searched for the right words. "This is weird for me too, but your husband is in trouble and I can't even imagine what you are going through. I'd like to try to help if I can."

"That's really kind. How do you know T.S.?"

Mary decided the truth was too hard to explain and would probably be misconstrued. "Your husband found my name in a legal directory and called me from the jail. I'm a lawyer, but not the right kind to help him for this. But we did talk for a while and I guess he felt comfortable calling me back when he needed to find help for you."

"I can't afford to pay you, ma'am."

"Oh, for goodness sake, I should've made that clear, sorry. I'm not looking to get paid. Really just want to help, is all."

Mary breathed through the palpable silence.

Mary continued with, "The least I can do is let you stay here for one night if you'd like. I know this was a rushed trip and you didn't have time to make any arrangements. At this time of night it'd be very hard for you to find a room, so if you're ok with it I'll come to the airport and pick you up and bring you here. In the morning we can work on a more permanent solution."

Edith was taken aback, nervous, and at the same time relieved. "I don't even know this woman," she thought to herself. And then in the face of the grim reality she thought, "But it doesn't matter much at this point. These are the cards I've been dealt."

Edith replied, "I would be very much obliged. Your kindness is unbelievable. I'm so grateful."

"Alright then. I should be there in about 25 minutes. Are you getting checked bags?"

"No. I have my carry on and that's it."

"OK. I'll call again when I'm just outside baggage claim. What are you wearing?"

"I'm pulling a black duffel bag and wearing a green Boston Celtics t-shirt."

"That's easy enough. I'll see you soon."

"Thank you again, so much."

"Alright."

As the two hung up the phone, the guard at the County jail slipped a small piece of paper under the door of the Brit's cell. He was wide awake and saw it right away. He jumped up and picked it off of the floor and nervously unfolded it. He read the penciled scribble, "Call from Attorney Roys. She got your message. Will take care of it."

T. S. crumpled the paper in his hand and closed his eyes in relief.

Chapter 21

Mary pulled out of her driveway and backed onto the dark, empty street. She put the car in drive and headed for the airport. She was wide awake now. Lost in thought, the trip seemed to take no time.

As she drove underneath the large green sign that said Arriving Flights she reached for her phone and used her call log to redial Edith. She put the phone against her ear.

"Hello?"

"Hello, Edith. This is Mary and I am just pulling into the airport. Can you look at the signs and let me know which section of baggage claim I should look for?"

Edith looked and saw the sign. "Baggage Claim C," she said.

"OK. Great. I should be pulling around in just a minute. Is it crowded where you are?"

"No. I'm practically by myself."

"Good. It should be a piece of cake to spot you. See you in a sec," and she hung up.

Mary slowed down and started to look for the

woman in the Celtics t-shirt. She passed slowly by Baggage Claim B and then she saw her. She pulled over to the curb and put on her emergency flashers. She hopped out of the car and around to the curb.

"Edith?"

"Yes. Mary?"

"Yes."

There was a short silence which Mary broke, "Well, come on then. Let's get you back to my place and you can rest from your long trip."

"Oh, thank you so much," Edith said as she put her bag into the trunk of Mary's car. "I can't believe you are doing this for me."

"It's nothing, Edith. Really, it's nothing."

Edith sat down in the passenger seat and pulled the seat belt around her shoulder and latched it. Mary did the same on the driver's side. She glanced into the side view mirror and pulled out.

Mary looked sideways to Edith and assessed her. She was very attractive in a plain way. She had flip flops on with pinstriped gray suit pants and a white blouse with two buttons undone. From the side Mary could see her breast through the opening of her shirt. Edith had short blond hair, which surprised Mary. Her wedding ring was modest.

Edith stared out the window and Mary wanted to put at her at ease if she could.

"Was the flight OK?"

Edith turned quickly to look at her, obviously relieved that she had broken the silence.

"Yes, quite. No problems."

And Edith smiled to herself and Mary noticed.

"Something funny?"

"Funny no," said Edith, "but it's certainly a stretch for me to be saying there are no problems." She turned her head away and started to cry softly.

"This must be so hard," Mary said. "I can't even imagine."

"Hard, yes. Very hard indeed."

Mary hesitated and thought before she spoke next. She did not want to push too hard too fast.

"I suppose it's none of my business but what do

you know about what's happening with your husband?"

Edith smiled. "Well, first off I suppose T.S. and I have made it your business by imposing on you this way. So please don't even think about apologizing for asking why you're driving a stranger to your house tonight," and she smiled warmly at Mary.

"OK," Mary said, and she was starting to like Edith.

"As for what I know, frighteningly little I dare say. My husband called and told me he was under arrest for murder and we had to end the call right about the time I was asking him for the details on what happened. For me, it is an unbelievable reality. I have no idea what happened, how it happened, why it happened. Do you?"

"I'm afraid not Edith."

Mary stopped hard at a light that just turned red. "Sorry," she said as the car lurched to a stop. "I guess I should pay more attention to driving."

"That's alright."

The light turned green and the car moved forward

before they spoke again.

"How do I go and see him?" Edith asked.

"You know, I'm not really sure. I'll call the jail in the morning and find out. Being a lawyer will at least get me to the right people. We'll call first thing and iron all that out. Have you eaten?"

"Yes, thank you. And I don't suppose I needed to. I have no appetite. I'm not sure if I have any sense of any feeling. Just a desire to go to sleep and wake up and find out it's all a dream."

Mary reached over and touched Edith on her left forearm. It was her way of saying "I understand."

"We'll be to my place in just a minute. Try to just rest and relax if you can. I guess all of this talk is not helping."

Edith turned and looked at Mary. "This talk is just what I need."

Edith closed her eyes and tilted her head back.

Mary pulled into her driveway. She looked over at Edith and in a manner of seconds she had fallen asleep. Mary hit the remote to open the garage door and pulled the car forward. She tapped Edith on the arm to wake her. Edith slowly opened her eyes and for a brief moment had a look as if to say "where am I?"

She came to, and quickly back to reality.

"Whew," she said. "I dozed off."

"Good for you," Mary said. "Let's get your bag and get you inside to bed."

Edith eased out of the passenger side and tried to grab the bag away from Mary. Mary refused politely and insisted on bringing the bag to Edith's room. She invited Edith in and asked her to sit in the living room while she got her room ready. Edith sat on the couch and closed her eyes. She did not sleep.

Mary bounded down the stairs and said, "Alright, then. Everything is ready. It's late and I know you're very tired. We have a lot to do tomorrow so how about we both get some rest."

"That sounds good. And thanks again for this. But for you I would be very lost right now, in a foreign country, a strange city, and in a world of serious trouble. You're a real angel."

"Enough," Mary said. "Off to bed with you. First room on the right at the top of the stairs."

Mary watched Edith go up the steps and turn right and out of sight into the guest room. She flipped off the lights and went to her room. Despite all of the unusual excitement, both were asleep within minutes.

Chapter 22

It was Friday morning in Las Vegas. Bob Scotti was at his desk early, reviewing files. There were more cases in front of him than he could possibly take to trial. He rubbed his forehead and stretched his neck muscles. It seemed too early to have a tension headache.

"Bob," said a voice over the speaker phone. "You in there?"

Bob pressed the talk button on the intercom and answered the secretary who worked for at least five public defenders, "Yeah, I'm here. What's up?"

"The DA's office just delivered the surveillance tape from the casino. For the murder case with the British guy. Should I bring it in?"

Bob looked over his calendar and said, "Sure, let me have a quick look." He tossed the manila envelope aside and rolled his chair over to his computer.

She opened the door and tossed the DVD on his desk without coming into the room and without saying a word.

Bob put the DVD into his laptop and booted up the tapes. He fast forwarded to a point where his client was at a table with the victim. Just as he started to watch the deal for a hand of poker with the Brit sitting right next to the victim the phone rang. Bob paused the video, at a point where it was a full close up on the Brit peering at his cards under his cupped hand. He could see from the caller ID that it was the DA's office so he picked it up.

"Bob?"

"Yeah, this is Bob. Is that you Del?"

"Yeah. How's everything on the dark side?"

"I don't know. I was just about to ask you the same thing," and they both chuckled.

"Bob I wanted you to know that I've been assigned to the Fowler case and I got word you were on it from your end."

"That's right. I actually had a note here to call you later this morning. Funny, because I just started watching the casino surveillance video when you called."

"Save your time Bob. Use your imagination on your other cases. With this one it's time to play

Let's Make a Deal."

"Cocky," Bob replied, and when Del did not respond he said, "OK. I'm listening. But why should fast forward to the plea bargain?"

Del sat back in his chair and put his feet on his desk, "Bob, this is over and done. We have the guy red handed. We have robbery as the motive. We have a hotel invasion aka a burglary. We have everything we need to press hard for first degree murder, felony or premeditated." He paused for emphasis and said, "And we can hang, no pun intended, the death penalty over this poor shit's head. Do you wanna watch the video or do you wanna talk about saving this poor guy's ass?"

"Maybe the video can wait. What're you thinking?"

"Well, I'm thinking we go on Monday… Oh, I forgot to mention that the arraignment is on Monday before Judge Lanham," Bob stopped, smiled to himself, and waited for the response.

"Jesus Christ! Lanham. Why me?"

"Good clean living I guess, but that's the card you drew from the deck."

"Shit."

"Shit squared." Del knew he was in business. "Anyway, back to what I'm thinking. The best I should offer is second degree with a definite term of 25 and parole after 10, with a prospective recommendation of parole at 10 assuming no fuck ups from your guy in the joint. That's really the best I should do, and that would be cutting to the chase. That would normally be a take it or leave it proposition? Can we be clear on that?"

"I hear what you're saying, but why the equivocation?"

"Hear me out."

"OK, but what about self-defense? My guy says the other guy attacked him."

Dell was pissed. "Because I could go in and win a second degree with my eyes closed and a jury made up of the Liverpool soccer team for Christ's sake. Give me a fucking break Bob."

There was a pregnant pause.

Del went on, "You almost just fucked this up." He composed himself, looking at his jammed calendar and a hopeless caseload. "You were good to me in that gangbanger deal. Goddamn reasonable. I've been waiting for a chance to return the favor. So if your guy agrees today, I'll go the extra mile and offer voluntary manslaughter with a 5 year term and the possibility of parole after 2 years."

He waited for a reaction.

When he didn't get one he continued, "I get a conviction and close a file, you're a hero for getting such a sweet deal, and our man spends some time in jail, gets out, goes back to England and doesn't hurt anybody else in the States."

Bob was stunned at the leniency of the offer but tried to play it cool.

"I can't be sure how we want to go until I talk to my guy. I'll do what I can. What time are we on for Monday?"

"First out of the box at 9:00. I'm available until 5:00 today Bob, but after that I can't promise you anything."

"Understood. Can you email me the arraignment notice for the file?"

"Sure thing. Hitting the send button now. Let's talk before 5:00 OK? I'd like to enjoy a weekend for a change."

"I'll see what I can do. I expect we'll have a deal by 5:00."

And they both hung up the phones without anything further.

Bob hit the speaker button and called over to the jail.

"Bob Scotti here."

"Yeah, Mr. Scotti. Hal here. What can I do you for?"

"I need to arrange another interview with Fowler. Can you make that happen for 11:00?"

Hal checked over the coffee stained calendar on his desk.

"I can. We'll see you then. I'll have Fowler ready for you."

"Thanks, Hal."

Edith woke up around 8:15. She looked at the clock beside her bed and jumped up startled that she had slept so late. She pulled off the covers and put her feet on the floor. She took a deep breath and tried to get her bearings and her wits about her. "Is this really happening," she thought to herself.

Edith walked into the kitchen. Mary was at the table sipping coffee and reading the morning newspaper. She looked up and said, "Well, there she is. Good morning. I assume you slept ok?"

"Good morning ma'am. Slept too good I'm afraid. I really wanted to be up earlier. And I don't want to intrude on your normal schedule. What about your work?"

"I work too hard already and I deserve a Friday off. So today is Friday and I am off, as of 45 minutes ago when I decided."

"I'm dreadfully sorry to keep you from your work. I am really embarrassed."

"Don't be. One day away from what I do won't have any impact on the world. Coffee?"

"I don't suppose you have any tea?"

"I do. It might not meet your standards, but there is some in the pantry. Have a look and help yourself. I'll put on some water."

"Thanks," Edith said as she disappeared around the corner and into the walk-in pantry.

Mary filled a kettle from the kitchen faucet and called into her, "When do you want to arrange for a visit with your husband?"

Edith popped her head around the corner. "I suppose as soon as I can."

"Fix your tea and I'll start making some calls."

Mary left Edith in the kitchen and went into the small study off of her living room. She thought about who to call first. She decided to call directly to the jail. Edith sipped her tea and stared into space. She could hear Mary talking on the phone but she couldn't make out anything of what she was saying. "What must it be like for T. S.?" she thought. "How could he survive jail?" She had seen the prison shows on TV. "What was happening to him in there?" She started to form a mental image and she began to feel sick.

Mary bounced back into the room and snapped Edith out of her malaise. "Alright. So we can go over at around 10:00 and we - and by "we" I mean you - should get to see your husband for about 20 minutes. I understand he's meeting with his lawyer at 11:00 so he'll be having a busy morning. Now why don't you get in the shower and get ready. I'll drive you over. While you're in the shower I'll fix you some breakfast," and as Mary could sense that Edith would resist eating she plowed on, "and no is not an option. You have to eat because you have to be strong; for you and for him."

"Alright, ma'am. You're right. But please don't go to too much trouble."

"What trouble? You like frozen waffles?"

"My absolute favorite, they are" and they both laughed.

Judge Lanham had taken Friday off too. He was at home killing time while he waited for his friends to pick him up for a golf game. They had a 10:48 tee time and the judge was antsy, looking forward to it.

He was surfing the cable TV stations and landed on a morning news show with a picture of the President and the British Prime Minister holding a press conference in the Rose Garden at the White House. The judge stopped surfing and turned up the volume. As he listened his face grew red and his fists clenched.

The judge listened as the morning talking heads explained that the British Prime Minister was rejecting a request from the United States to conduct a full inquiry into the release by Great Britain to Libya of the infamous Lockerbie bomber. He fumed as he listened to allegations that the release was tied to potential oil exploration in Libya by a British oil conglomerate. He nearly threw his coffee cup when he listened to the report that the prisoner had been freed for "humanitarian" reasons after serving only 8 years of a life sentence. He watched the video of the prisoner walking feebly to a plane in London with a handkerchief over his face, and then watched the video of the same guy deplaning in Tripoli, bounding down the stairs and hugging the dignitaries lined up to greet him as a hero.

"Sons of bitches," he muttered to himself. "Sons of mother fucking bitches." He went to get his blood pressure monitor.

The Brit was finishing breakfast in the mess hall when a guard told him he would be getting a visit from his wife at 10:00. He momentarily lost his breath.

The Brit was returned to his cell. His mind raced now in anticipation of the meeting. How would he explain all of this? How could he face her with his shame and his guilt? How would she react? What if she was here to say goodbye forever? Could he blame her? What would she do while he sat in jail and went through a trial and laid his fate at the feet of twelve strangers from a foreign country? Could he even ask her to wait? Could he even ask her for forgiveness and understanding? Should he let her go and encourage her to find a new life with someone worthy of her? What kind of man could do this to a sweet woman like her? What kind of man was he? Questions were racing through his mind in rapid succession. Answers were few and far between.

As he thought about the upcoming meeting it occurred to him that the last 48 hours seemed like 48 years. He could not really remember playing poker in the room in the Las Vegas casino. That seemed such a distant and foggy memory. He did not remember the killing, the arrest, the aftermath – that all seemed like a vague and far off dream. He was, however, quite in the moment. He was in jail in Las Vegas, Nevada, and he did not have a get out of jail free card.

Now, as he waited to meet with his wife, time stood absolutely still. It did not move at all. He was stuck in time, fixed in position, and unable to move physically or mentally or emotionally or spiritually. He remembered what the poet, his namesake, once said, "I don't believe one grows older. I think that what happens early on in life is that at a certain age one stands still and stagnates."

Finally, the Brit heard the familiar footsteps coming down the hall. It was time.

The Brit had dry mouth and was so nervous he was shaking as he walked toward the visiting center. He was led into a large room with stark tables and benches. At the far end of the room, sitting quietly and looking quite out of place and scared, was Edith. He never saw a more welcome site.

She had on a striped fisherman's shirt that was a Chanel knockoff. Her hair was pulled back into a bun and her eyes looked tired. She stood when she saw him coming, and he could tell from her expression that the shock of seeing him in an orange prison jumpsuit was very real. Try as she might, she could not hide the horror she was feeling in greeting her husband, the prisoner, the murderer. They sat across from each other, no physical contact was allowed, and his handcuffs would stay on.

Neither spoke until the guard had moved away.

"Thank god you are here Edith. Thanks to

almighty god."

"I am here love. I'm here."

The Brit looked down at his cuffed hands and clasped the ends of his fingers together. He looked up at his wife before he spoke.

"Edith, I don't have any bloody idea what to say. I'm so terribly ashamed and so horribly sorry to drag you through this. I keep thinking that I will snap out of it and it'll all be a bad dream occasioned by some bad booze, but I know it's real." He looked down again at his hands, at the iron around his wrists, and then back up again at her. "How can it be real?"

"It's real enough, love," she said, averting her eyes toward the floor.

"I wish I could touch you Edith. I wish I could hold you. I wish we could leave now and start all over again."

"I know, T. S.," she said, "me too."

She broke the brief lull in the conversation, "So what do we do now?"

"I don't know Edith. Honest to god I don't know. How are you holding up? What must you think of me? How can you ever look at me the same way as before?"

"I don't know that I've had time to think of any of that. The past two days seem like a complete blur. The roundabout needs to stop so I can catch my breath and think a straight thought. So far I'm reeling."

"Have you plans for the next few days? Do you know how long you will stay or where you will stay or how you will get by?"

"I don't have plans beyond the middle of this meeting, love. I've never been so completely immersed into any one moment. I scarcely know what the word plan means at this point."

"It's the same for me. I am dazed."

They looked at each other. How was this happening?

T.S. spoke first again.

"I'm meeting with my lawyer at 11:00. I'm sure he'll help with the immediate legal plans. I'm so lost in all of it. It would be hard enough to understand if I wasn't in a panic, but in my state it's completely incomprehensible. I just hope he knows what he's doing."

"I am sure he does, love."

"Listen, Edith, we don't have too much more time so I wanted to tell you something, ok? I want to talk about what happens when we finally get through this mess."

"OK. But define getting through this."

"I can't right off. But it must be our premise for now."

"Alright. I'll presume being through this, as foreign a concept as that is to me right now."

"I know it's hard love, but thank you."

"Go on T.S."

"I was fretting horribly about what to say to you. I was dismayed, wrestling with my thoughts. Then it hit me."

"What hit you, T.S.?"

"That we have run into a wall in life. That we are frozen as people, as a couple, and that we are in a time warp. We are not necessarily getting older, we are just treading water. It is my fault, and dare I say yours as well. I've been doing a lot of thinking about what happened to us. How we got to where we are – not this I mean – but how we got to where we are generally in life and particularly in our marriage. Eliot said it best, "People to whom nothing has ever happened cannot understand the unimportance of events."

"I don't understand."

"You see, Edith, before this mess we thought little things were important because nothing ever really happened to us. Something has happened to us Edith. It's a big thing and a bad thing, but it's something. We should focus on the importance of life and not of events."

The Brit paused and for a brief moment he closed his eyes. When he opened them he said, "I need to get through this to make things right with you. Is it fair for me to ask you to see this through with me?"

"Fair may be a poor choice of words, but whatever it is I have little choice. I'm with you T.S. God knows that I don't see the other side of this yet, but I am with you."

"Bless you Edith and thank god for your strength and your comfort. If we do get through this I promise that I'll be a new man, a husband worthy of a gem like you. I do see some light at the end of this terribly dark tunnel."

"We'll see T.S. But best to take this a step at a time, don't you think?"

The guard approached and gave the warning that time was almost up.

Edith said, "I'll come as often as I can."

"I love you Edith," and the Brit began to tear up.

"I know you do, dear. Me too."

He blew her a kiss as the guard pulled him up by his elbow. She feigned a kiss back and waved until he was out of sight. The door slammed loudly behind him.

Chapter 23

The Brit barely had time to stop reeling from the meeting with his wife when the guard returned to fetch him for the meeting with the public defender.

"Good morning, T. S.," said Bob. "How are you?"

"Better, sir. I saw my wife this morning and that's really helped, all things being considered of course."

"Good. Glad to hear that. I asked to see you because I've had a productive morning too. First, your arraignment is Monday morning at 9:00. Like we talked about the other day, remember; that's when you have to enter your plea."

"My god," said the Brit, "that leaves very little time to think. Such a crucial decision, isn't it?"

"Normally I would agree," Bob said. "But I had a very interesting talk with the district attorney this morning and he's offering a very attractive deal, one that's almost too good to be true."

"What deal?"

"In a nutshell, you're at real high risk for getting nailed with a first degree murder charge. Granted it would be hard for the state to prove premeditation – not impossible, just difficult – but in Nevada it is first degree murder if the killing is during a robbery or an attempted robbery. That fits here. They have a solid case that you broke into the hotel room to steal the money you lost at the tables. If we go to trial and they make that stick, you get hit with first degree."

"I know that's bad, but how bad?"

"Death by lethal injection for starters." Bob paused to let that sink in. "Of course that's worst case and unlikely, but how lucky are you feeling? Best case is a prison term of 50 years with a first chance for parole after 20. Most likely result, a life sentence with a chance of parole after 20. Any way you slice it, assuming you stay alive, you have 20 years in state prison."

"Holy shit."

"Precisely."

The Brit was very pale.

"You think this place sucks? The state big house is hell on earth."

Bob paused to let the Brit imagine prison.

Bob went on, "Even if they can only make a second degree murder charge stick you're looking at either life with a chance of parole after 10 years or a term of 25 years with a chance of parole after 10. Either way you get at least 10 years."

"So what is the DA's offer?"

"A guilty plea to a voluntary manslaughter charge with a recommended sentence of 5 years and a chance for parole after 2. He owed me a favor, and this is a huge one."

The Brit leaned back and took a deep breath. "What do you think?"

"I think you better authorize me to call and accept that deal before the DA sobers up."

"Can I talk to my wife about it?"

"Only if you can talk to her before 5:00 today. The offer expires then."

"Does it have to move that fast?"

Bob glared at him, losing patience immediately. "No, it doesn't. We could enter a not guilty plea on Monday and the DA could get some other cases resolved, change his mind, or get a wild hair up his ass for British guys. Who knows what he might do. And all of a sudden he queers this fucking deal. And I could make like Perry fucking Mason and spend a lot of time looking at tapes, interviewing witnesses, analyzing the forensic evidence, all of that shit. And at the end of the day we are right back to a fucking whack on the head in a hotel room with a poor son of a bitch from Kentucky bleeding to death on the floor." Bob tried to calm down. He took a breath. He lowered his voice. "I'm telling you that in this case under these circumstances you need to jump at this deal now and we need to have it in the can for Monday morning. You can't do better than this. No fucking way, no fucking how."

The Brit stood and paced. "I can't make a decision to go away for 5 years without talking with Edith."

"OK. Look," Bob said, "where is she?"

"Staying with Mary Roys. She's an attorney in town but I don't know where she lives. I have her office number."

"I can find the number. Here's what we need to do. You authorize me to take this deal on the condition that I try to speak with your wife before this afternoon. OK? The other question is what do you want me to do if I can't find her by then? I need to know your plan B, because if you don't take this deal I'm going to paper the fuck out of my file so it's crystal clear you didn't listen to my advice. I'm not going to be answering to a claim of ineffective assistance of counsel because you have 50 fucking years on your hands in the prison law library. Understand? I been down that fucking road before."

"Yeah," the Brit said softly. "I do understand." He bit his lower lip. "Give me five minutes alone."

"Sure," and Bob stepped out to get a soft drink.

The Brit was calculating fast and furiously. He killed the man. He broke into the hotel room to steal the money. He had no factual defense. He could not win. He knew exactly what he was doing when he went for that money. And he knew it was wrong. Bob was right. This was a very good deal. He could hope for no prison, but hope would not produce an outcome. As his head started to hurt very badly he recalled the Eliot line, "Humankind cannot bear very much reality."

The Brit decided what to do in less than two minutes. For the better part of three more minutes he waited for Bob to return.

Bob pushed open the door and stuck his head in,

"Well?" He walked in and closed the door.

"OK. Please try to talk with Edith and explain the situation. But one way or the other get that deal today before it expires."

"You're a smart man, T. S., a smart man. I'll get you a message when it's done," and as he went to leave he turned abruptly and said, "Oh, one more thing. Any plea deal is subject to the judge accepting it, but that's almost never a problem and I don't anticipate one here. Just need to tell you that to cover my ass. I'll be in touch."

The Brit was alone and staring straight into the face of a prison sentence. Would Edith wait for him? How could he ever know while he was in a Nevada prison and she was living freely in London? An attractive woman like her would have lots of attention. How could she wait for a man who was never all that good to her to begin with? In the end, though, the Brit knew that he had no choice but to play this hand.

Bob went back to his office and asked his secretary to find the number for a Mary Roys, a civil attorney somewhere in Las Vegas. By lunch time, Bob had a number. After going through her office and several roadblocks to getting her home number, Bob was dialing her up.

Bob left three messages on the home phone number for Mary Roys. At 4:15 he couldn't wait any longer. He called Del and made the deal for the Brit. It would be presented to the judge for approval on Monday.

Just before 5:00 Bob used his contacts at the jail to transmit the following scribbled message to his client: "Done deal. See you Monday morning."

At 5:25 Mary and Edith returned to Mary's home. She listened to the messages and called the public defender's office immediately. Everyone was gone for the weekend.

Chapter 24

Edith arrived at the jail around 10:30 Saturday morning for her second visit with her husband. She met him in the same room as the day before, at the table and bench just next to the one they had used for their first meeting.

"Good morning, love," she said, trying to be cheery.

"Morning Edith," he said, "how was your night?"

"Just fine for me but really let's talk about you – how are you doing in here?"

"I'm holding up Edith. They have me in isolation so I don't really have to worry too much about the others so far. Did my lawyer get hold of you yesterday?"

"No. Mary and I got back to her place after business hours and there was a message but we never hooked up. What did he want?"

The Brit explained the plea bargain and the process as best as he could. He told Edith that if everything went as expected he may be in prison for only 2 years and that as it had been explained to him that was as good as he could expect.

Edith listened and tried to take it all in. She moved to the subject that had been on her mind but still untouched, "You know I still don't know what the hell happened here T.S. If you are going to plead guilty to this any way I see no harm in telling me what happened just so I can have a little peace of mind that you are not a raving lunatic killer."

"You're right love. No harm at all."

The Brit started at the beginning and he didn't leave out any details so long as he remembered them. He explained his ups and downs at the table and how he had lost everything in a horrible bit of bad luck and that he simply lost his sense of rationality and followed the man from Kentucky up to his room. He described the feeling – the urge – to get that money back at all costs. He tried as best he could to explain how in the back of his head he knew none of it could work but that these pangs of reasonableness did not dampen his enthusiasm for getting that money – his money – back.

The Brit tried to remember and recount in detail the moments leading up to the end. He felt very uneasy as he described the dull blow he landed on the man's head with the heavy lamp. And he felt as if he would be ill when he described the feeling when the hotel security opened the door and caught him standing over the man from Kentucky, wiping blood from the hotel room door handle.

She was aghast as she listened. She did not ask any questions. She did not interrupt him. She was simply aghast.

When he finished the story by summarizing his trip to the jail and the booking, he dropped his head down and waited for his wife to say something.

She was stunned and confused. How could this man who never hurt a fly kill a man? How could he have been so moved to take such a ridiculous course of action? How could their lives ever be anywhere near the same again?

"I don't know what to say T.S. I really need to have some time for all of this to soak in."

"I know love. What can I say? Somehow I'm sorry seems to fall very short."

"What will we do?" she asked, with no expectation of an answer.

"It is hard. It will be hard. But I think if you can wait for me – god knows I don't deserve that - but if you can wait for me we can start a new life in 2 years, worst off 5. We can be alive again. We can break free from the stagnation. We can stop hiding behind a pair of cards face down on a velvet green table. We can crawl out of our addictions and make something real for ourselves. What do you think love? Please say you'll wait. Please say we can live again."

Edith was crying. She could not decide whether she was sad, depressed, happy, or confused.

"I still think for now it's got to be a day at a time T.S. It is all much too much for me. I need to go a day at a time for now. You understand don't you?"

"Of course, love. I'm in no position to not understand. I'm just happy you're willing to go it at all – and a day at a time is as much as I can reasonably ask for. But I'm serious, love. This is a horrible wakeup call for me, a real wakeup call."

The two spent the rest of the visit talking about less serious things – the food in jail, the weather outside, how Edith was getting on with Mary. Because there were no Sunday visitations, this Saturday visit lasted almost an hour and a half.

Just before noon the guard came and got the Brit. For the second time in as many days Edith watched him walk back into a world she could only imagine, in an orange jumpsuit with large black stenciled letters back and front – INMATE.

Mary was waiting for Edith in a coffee shop just down the street. She was checking emails and voice mails on her cell phone and hardly noticed Edith until she was sitting at the table.

"Hey," Mary said, "how'd it go?"

"Fine. We talked about a lot of things including what happened…"

Mary cut her off. "No, wait just a minute. Don't tell me anything about what happened. OK. It's better for me to not know."

"OK. I understand Mary. I won't. So, beside that we talked about something called a plea bargain."

"Now that's something I'd like to hear about. Is that why the PD was trying to call you yesterday?"

"I suppose so."

"Did your husband tell you what the offer is?"

"Yeah, he did. And he said his lawyer is telling him to jump at it before it disappears."

"What is it?" Mary said, sitting up and putting her

elbows on the table.

"I'm pretty sure he said a plea of guilty to voluntary murder, or something like that?"

"Voluntary manslaughter?"

"Yeah, that's it," and she paused. "What a vile term – manslaughter."

Mary became more interested, "OK. That's not bad." She paused, thinking. "Did he say anything about the recommended sentence?"

"5 years with I think he said eligibility for parole after 2?"

"Not bad at all." Mary picked up her coffee cup and took a small sip. "It makes me suspicious. Why would the DA roll over like that so soon?"

Mary put down the coffee cup and no one spoke while she thought.

After about 45 seconds Mary went on, "OK, no details. But just tell me whether it sounds like a jury could decide he didn't do it."

"No, not likely."

"How about that he was provoked or that he was

acting in self-defense, anything like that?"

"No. It sounds bad Mary, real bad."

"Hmmm," Mary muttered, "then it seems too good to be true."

"Do you think there's something fishy Mary?"

"I don't know. But I'd like to talk to the PD tomorrow if I can get him."

"Would you Mary? That would be so helpful."

"Yes, Edith. I'll try. I promise I will try."

Edith looked down at her watch and changed the topic, "How about some lunch?"

"For the first time in days I actually think I would like to eat," Edith said.

"Good," Mary said, "let's go get something at my golf club – it is quiet, private and we can sit outside under an umbrella and have a glass of wine and pretend none of this is happening."

"That sounds grand, Mary," and then she stopped in her tracks and grabbed Mary by the arm, "but I can't keep imposing on you like this. I need to find a place to stay. I have to get out of your hair."

Mary turned and looked at her. She took Edith's hand, "It would make me happy if you would stay with me for as long as you like."

Edith started to interrupt but Mary put up one finger to shush her. She went on, "It's not only for you Edith. It's making me feel good to help. Stay with me for me, and we both win, that is unless you want to go somewhere else."

Edith looked back at Mary. She cocked her head to the side as if to say "I don't understand but I believe you."

Then Edith said out loud, "Really?"

"Really, Edith," Mary said softly. "Really." They reached out to each other for a hug. They pulled apart slowly.

"Well, that's settled then. I'll stay with you on the condition that you will tell me when you change your mind and on the further non-negotiable condition that I pull my weight by cooking, cleaning, and generally being a good roommate. Are we agreed?"

"Agreed."

They smiled warmly at each other

"I'm starving," Mary said.

"So let's eat," said Edith as she pulled Mary by the arm in the direction of the car.

Chapter 25

"I can't believe that son of a bitch never called me back," Mary said to Edith as they drove toward the County Courthouse.

"All I can do is keep thanking you for trying Mary."

It was 8:35 Monday morning and the two did not want to be late for the arraignment. Mary had already explained that going to court was all about hurrying up and then waiting, but they could not take a chance that a proceeding might actually start on time. Mary parked the car in the lot across the street from the courthouse.

Judge Lanham sat in his chambers reading the morning newspaper. His clerk walked in with a stack of files.

"Morning Judge," he said as he placed the files in the middle of his desk.

"Morning, Jimmy. How was your weekend?"

"Not bad, Judge. I went fishing with my grandson and we had a real good time. Caught the limit in half a day. How about you?"

"Played golf on Friday and took money from all

the boys. A real good round. Spent some time with my daughter on Saturday and yesterday the wife and I just meandered around doing some work in the yard. Pretty relaxing really."

"Sounds good."

"Yeah, it was." He pulled his reading glasses from his head and laid them on the desk. He put his head in his hand and spoke softly. "But here we go again. The start of another week in judicial paradise." He looked up and grunted. "What do we have this morning Jimmy?

"Three arraignments, it looks like. Here are the files. Two pleas and one plea bargain."

"Put the pleas first and we'll do the bargain last. What's the deal?"

"Murder case. Some British guy…" and the Judge interrupted.

"British guy, huh? Look at this shit Jimmy," and he pointed his large index finger at the article just below the fold on the front page about the Lockerbie bomber. "British fuckers are not being real cooperative with us right now Jimmy."

"I see that sir," Jimmy said.

"Not very cooperative at all."

The Judge stood up and put on his robes. He took one last long drink of the lukewarm black coffee and said, "Call this shit to order Jimmy. Let's get on with it so we can each have a little time for ourselves before lunch. We pick up that rape trial again this afternoon. Fuck."

Jimmy stepped out and whispered to the court reporter to make sure she was ready to go. "All rise," he said, and everyone did. "The Eighth Judicial District Court of Clark County is now in session. The honorable Judge George Lanham presiding."

As the judge took the bench he said, "Be seated."

"Call the first case," the judge said.

Jimmy stood up and read from the docket sheet. "The State of Nevada v. Elisa Ramm."

The Brit sat in the second row, handcuffed and in his orange jumpsuit, with Bob Scotti by his side. Bob's adversary was handling all three arraignments this morning so he was at counsel table addressing the court and listening to the presentment of the indictment against Ms. Ramm.

Edith and Mary sat in the last row, on the side of

the courtroom behind the Brit.

It was 9:55 when Jimmy said, "The State of Nevada v. T. S. Fowler."

Bob took the Brit by the arm and led him to the counsel table for the defense. Del was still at the podium from the previous arraignment and he stayed there until the judge spoke.

"Mr. District Attorney I see there's a proposed plea bargain in this case, is that right?"

"Yes, your honor. If it please the court I have filed a plea memorandum in consultation with Mr. Scotti. It just needs your signature."

The judge flipped through the papers in the file before him. He glanced over at the newspaper article about the British Prime Minister. He looked back through the plea papers, paging through them slowly as he thought.

"Let me take a look here," the judge said.

"Mr. Fowler," the judge bellowed.

Bob pulled the Brit up by the elbow.

"Yes, sir," the Brit said, surprised that the judge was addressing him.

"I need to make sure you understand exactly what you're doing here…"

Mr. Scotti rose and interrupted. "Your honor I have explained all of this to my client…"

Judge Lanham came part way out of his seat and shouted, "Sit down Mr. Scotti." His face was redder than Kansas on election day.

Bob slowly took his seat.

The judge was visibly upset and was straining for control. "Mr. Fowler?"

"Yes, sir."

"I understand that you're a gambler. Is that right?"

"Yes, sir. I play poker."

"Do you understand how this case got assigned to me?"

"No, sir. I'm afraid I don't."

"Random draw, Mr. Fowler, random draw. There are eight judges in this county who handle criminal matters, and you got me."

"I see, sir."

"And most judges in this county rubber stamp these plea deals. Did you know that?"

"No, sir. I did not."

"Well, one judge doesn't and you're looking at him now. So let's chat about this deal, shall we?"

Del and Bob knew Lanham was a wild card but this was going beyond what they had seen and certainly not what they expected.

"If you like, sir."

"Mr. Scotti here interrupted me a minute ago and I assume he was going to pat himself on the back by telling me had given you a full explanation of what this deal is and how this whole process works. Do you think I'm right about that?"

"I can't say sir. He has explained it to me though." The Brit's voice was shaking.

"Let's talk about the deal and then I'm going to tell you a few things that Mr. Scotti probably didn't tell you, ok?"

Edith looked over at Mary. Mary shot a look back that clearly showed her concern. A slight nod of the head and purse of her lips said "I have no idea what is going on here."

The judge continued, "Do you know we have rules of criminal procedure here in Nevada? Those rules apply to everyone that comes before this court. Even you, a British citizen getting into a bit of a jam while on holiday. Is that how you'd say it in your country, a bit of a jam?"

The Brit looked at Bob who nodded his head ever so slightly to advise him not to respond.

"The court rules say that this little get together, we call it the initial appearance and arraignment, is the time when the court, that's me, and counsel, that's your friend Mr. Scotti and the district attorney here, take the opportunity to establish a meaningful schedule for the trial and the pretrial activity in the case."

The judge took a sip from his glass of water and looked out over his reading glasses to make sure everyone was paying attention. He placed the glass down.

"Humor me while we apply the rules before we get to your proposed agreement."

Mr. Scotti spoke, "Your honor, if I may?"

The Judge was pleased with the groveling

deference, "That's better counsel. Go ahead."

"My client waives presentment of the information under local rule 3."

"Thank you Mr. Scotti, that saves us a little time. As you know you have at least a 5 day extension for this proceeding if you want to take it given your appointment under local rule 3(a) (2). Do you want that?"

"No, your honor. We waive our right to the extension and we stand ready to proceed today."

"Very well. Do either of you want to discuss conditions for release or detention? Probably a waste of time with a clear flight risk, don't you think?"

Mr. Scotti responded, "Only if that's necessary after consideration of the plea bargain memorandum."

"OK. Let's get to that."

The judge pulled the memorandum from the file and started to read the label on the cover.

"So this is a plea to voluntary manslaughter?"

"Yes, your honor," the district attorney said.

"Voluntary manslaughter?" and the judge looked out at everyone over the tops of his reading glasses as if to say, "Are you shitting me?"

"Yes, your honor. If I could refer the court to page 2 of the memorandum." Del waited for the judge to get to the right place in the memorandum. "I have set out the factual basis for the plea agreement, the acknowledgement by counsel that the defendant has been advised of the discovery produced, and the evidence the State intends to produce at trial. I have also included a list of the factors that militate against proceeding to trial on higher charges."

The judge was reading.

"I see them counsel. But I am reading them over and over because I don't believe you filed this nonsense."

The judge turned to the Brit.

"Do you understand that you're waiving your right to a jury trial by entering this plea?"

"Yes, sir," the Brit said.

"Are you affirming to this court that you voluntarily consent to the terms of this plea agreement?"

"Yes, sir."

"Have you read this memorandum?"

"Yes, sir"

"Is this your signature on the memorandum?" and he held up the page for the Brit to see.

"Yes, sir."

"And did your esteemed counsel explain to you that under the laws of the State of Nevada the court, again that's me, is not bound by the plea bargain agreement?"

"Yes, Mr. Scotti did tell me that, but he said it wouldn't be a problem."

Scotti slumped down in his chair.

"Really?" Judge Lanham sat back in the big leather chair and puffed out his chest. "Is that what he told you, then?"

The Brit knew not to say any more.

"One final question, Mr. Fowler, before I render my decision. Did either of these lawyers tell you that the next time they bring a plea agreement like this before this court I will hold them in contempt? Did they tell you that? I bet not, but believe you me that is exactly what'll happen."

The judge threw down the memorandum and tried to catch his breath. He was sweating and he was flush.

"I bet you waive your right to a jury trial, Mr. Fowler. I bet you consent quite happily to this arrangement." The Judge raised his voice a notch. "I bet you signed this agreement, Mr. Fowler. I bet you couldn't wait to sign it. I bet Mr. Scotti here explained to you that this is the sweetest deal given to a Brit since the Stamp Act. I bet you thought you were going to leave today with a rubber stamp from me and a walk in the park. But you're charged with killing a man in my town over some poker chips, Mr. Fowler. And this deal is not justice. Not in the State of Nevada, not in the United States of America, and definitely not in my courtroom today."

The judge sipped some water and cleared his throat. He pushed his reading glasses back up onto the bridge of his nose.

"The court in the case of the State of Nevada v. Fowler rejects the plea bargain agreement presented and schedules a hearing for tomorrow morning at 9:00 for the purpose of entry of a plea by the defendant. And for no other purpose," he added, staring directly at the two lawyers he had just dressed down.

With that, the judge got up and stormed off of the bench.

He was through the door to his chambers before Jimmy finished saying, "All rise."

Jimmy picked up the files from the judge's desk and picked up the newspaper and folded it under his arm.

Judge Lanham ripped off his robes and sat down hard in his chair. "Fucking British," he muttered.

The Brit had no time to talk with Bob. The bailiff whisked him away and out toward the van waiting to take him back to jail. Bob called after him, "I'll stop by later to see you." As the Brit disappeared Bob dropped back down into his chair behind the defense table and hung his head.

Edith wept quietly in the back row. Mary held her arm around Edith's shoulders and rubbed her softly to console her. Del sat with a blank look and stared out the window. His mouth was open and he looked utterly stunned.

Bob started to move to put away his papers. Mary whispered to Edith, "Go get some air. I want to talk to your husband's lawyer in private."

Edith nodded and wiped the tears from her eyes with the tissue Mary had given her. She stood and walked out the double doors and into the courthouse hallway. She walked out the front door into the Nevada sunshine.

Mary watched her leave and then headed to the front of the courtroom to talk to Bob Scotti.

"Mr. Scotti?"

"Yes," he said.

She extended her hand, "Mary Roys, you tried to call me Friday. Your client's wife is staying with me."

"Oh, yeah. Hello," and he reached out to shake her hand. "Hey, sorry for not getting back to you over the weekend but I was away and didn't pick up messages until late last night."

"No problem," and then she got to the point. "What the fuck was that?" and she pointed to the empty bench.

Bob paused. "I have no idea. I've been doing this for a long time and I have never seen anything like it. I have to regroup to think about where to go from here."

"I'll say."

"I have to get to another meeting. Can you walk out with me?"

"Sure," she said. "Do you think you can do a plea for second degree?"

"Honestly, after that display Del is probably so puckered up he won't do anything but listen to us plead not guilty tomorrow morning. And the judge was pretty clear that he didn't want another memorandum."

"This really sucks."

"Yes, it does. Listen I really have to run. But please call me this afternoon when we can chat a little longer. Tell my client's wife I'm sorry. Damn, that would have been a good deal."

He walked out the door and passed by Edith without noticing her. Mary followed shortly behind and walked with Edith to their car.

Chapter 26

"We need to go somewhere and talk," Mary said to Edith as she put the key in the ignition.

Edith nodded.

"Hungry?"

Edith nodded no.

"Me either."

The engine turned over. "How about we take a drive to Horseman's Park and sit outside and collect our thoughts?"

Edith nodded. They drove without speaking.

May picked out a bench in the shade not far from a practice arena where reining horses were training for an upcoming show.

Mary sat and then Edith sat. They both watched the horses, one after the other, running through their patterns of small and big, slow and fast circles. They marveled at the long stops the horses made from full gallops. They watched in silence for almost 20 minutes. Edith spoke first.

"Well, now what? You said it was too good to be

true and it was."

Mary put her hand over eyes to shield the sun as she spoke.

"Well, since we're sort of brainstorming here, I guess we should put the possibility of an insanity defense on the table."

Edith cocked her head. "Insanity?"

"Yeah. It's a long shot. It's rarely used and even more rarely works. I'm not at all sure that we could bootstrap the facts of this case to fit."

"What is it? What does it mean?"

A horse walked by with a young man astride.

"Good afternoon ladies," he said.

They both nodded and smiled.

Mary explained, "There is an option in Nevada to plead not guilty by reason of insanity. In the simplest terms you're not saying you didn't do the crime, you're saying that you shouldn't be held criminally responsible because you lacked the mental capacity to understand that what you did was wrong. Did that make any sense at all?"

When Edith didn't say anything Mary went on,

"The other thing most people don't know is that the few people who succeed with the defense spend as much or more time in a mental institution as they would have spent in prison. And the judge retains control over your commitment. It's all kind of scary when you think about it."

"I'll say. Should T. S. consider it?"

"Based on what happened in court today he should be working on an escape plan."

Edith looked down at her watch. "Holy cow. It's almost 2:30."

"Shit. We need to go before you can't get into see him."

"Right. Let's go straight away."

"And while you are visiting with T.S. I'll look up our friend Mr. Scotti."

Chapter 27

As Mary and Edith talked in the park, the Brit was asleep in his cell having succumbed to the exhaustion of the morning and the previous sleepless night. He knew Bob was calling him at 4:00 and he wanted to get as much rest as possible before then.

"Get up in there, Fowler," yelled the guard.

The Brit sat up with a start. Sweat dripped from his hair.

"You're soaking wet, man," the guard said. He threw him a clean jump suit. "Get your ass changed and out here right away. Your lawyer is here and I'll be goddamned if I'm staying in this shithole past 5:30 on Monday night. I bowl tonight mother fucker."

"Be right with you," said the Brit as he quickly changed into his dry clothes.

"I thought you were going to call," said the Brit as he sat down across the table from Bob.

"I thought it might be better to talk face to face."

"What happened this morning?"

"I don't know exactly. I've seen Lanham go off before but that was completely out of the blue. The DA was just as shocked. None of us know what caused it or which Judge Lanham will show up tomorrow morning. But we have to regroup and develop a new plan."

"Aren't we running out of options?"

"Well, the best one was snatched from us so we have to start again and think about what we can do from here."

The Brit rubbed his eyes. He looked back at Bob with a look that clearly said "What do you think we should do?"

Bob fumbled with his papers and then started, "I haven't talked to the DA but we could go for a plea on second degree murder. We know the problems with that though: longer sentence and a judge who didn't look kindly on this plea. The DA may be gun shy."

"What if we just plead not guilty and see what happens?"

"That may be the only thing we can do."

They looked at each other for what seemed like a

very long time.

The Brit said, "But I'm guilty."

Bob stood up and walked in a small circle, brushing his hair back over his head with his right hand and scratching at the left side of his waist with the other. "I spoke briefly with your wife this afternoon."

"Yes? What did you talk about?"

"She and her lawyer friend were talking about the possibility of a not guilty by reason of insanity plea."

"They were, were they? And how exactly would that work, mate? I don't like the sounds of it one bit, I'll tell ya."

"It probably won't work at all, but it gives us some leverage with the court and the DA. It'll make them think about how much time and money it will take to deal with the psychiatric tests and the experts and the unsettled law in Nevada and maybe we work our way back around to a decent plea agreement. That is after Lanham gets back on his medication."

"But that means I would be saying that I'm

insane?"

"You'd be saying that you shouldn't be held criminally responsible because your act was caused by a mental condition."

"Same fucking thing, mate. Don't split hairs with me, alright?"

"OK. Take it easy. I'm just trying to work through a fairly fucked up situation here."

"I am sane. Do you hear me? I am sane. I have some fucking dignity left. I made a terrible mistake and I can't undo it, but I'll be goddamned if I'm going to say I'm not sane. Let's move on to our other options."

"I think you already hit on it. We plead not guilty tomorrow and see where things go from there."

"That's it then." And the Brit shut down. "I want to go back to my cell."

"Are you sure?" asked Bob. "Do you want to talk any more about tomorrow morning?"

"Fuck, tomorrow morning," the Brit said and he stood up to go to the door to call the guard. As he walked out with the guard pulling him along he turned and said, "And fuck you too."

Bob shook his head. "What a thankless job," he said. "And the pay sucks."

Bob walked onto the street and reached into his coat pocket for his cell phone. He dialed Mary Roy's number.

"Hello," Mary said.

"Mary, this is Bob Scotti."

"Hey, Bob. How did it go?"

"Not well at all. He has no interest in any defense that involves his sanity. He was really offended and pissed. Cut off our discussion and went back to his cell. Had a few choice words for me on the way out."

"I'm sorry to hear that. What now?"

"We plead not guilty tomorrow, start down the road to trial, and hope we get back to a plea bargain. I can't do anything else at this point."

"I guess that's right. I'll take care of telling his wife. If I come up with any brilliant ideas this evening I'll give you a call."

"Same here," he said, "but don't hold your

breath."

"See ya, Bob," she said and hung up.

Mary went into the living room where Edith was sitting and watching the evening news.

"That was your husband's lawyer, Edith," Mary said as she picked up the remote and switched off the TV.

"And?"

"And not good. T.S. got very upset at the idea of an insanity plea."

Edith sighed. "I should have known. T.S. has many shortcomings but lack of pride is not one."

"He's not leaving himself many good outs here."

"I know. But I'm afraid to push him on this." Edith put her head in her hands.

"You know him best, so I can't argue with you on that."

Edith pulled an afghan up around her knees. "I'm really beat Mary. Do you mind if I just veg out in front of the tellie tonight?"

"Of course not, Edith," she said. "I have plenty of

work to do. I'll be in my study if you need me."

"Thanks, Mary. You are a saint."

"Just get some rest, and call me in there if you need anything."

Edith turned the TV back on and Mary headed to her study. The Brit may give up and Edith may be close to giving up and maybe even Bob Scotti was ready to throw in the towel, but Mary was getting fired up.

She closed the study door and clicked on the desktop computer. Once it booted up she logged on to her online legal research account and scrolled through the search options and plugged in the search terms "insanity plea over defendant objection." She started to work.

Chapter 28

The TV was on but Edith was not watching it. She grabbed a pad of paper from the kitchen drawer and picked up a pen from the counter next to the refrigerator. She put on her reading glasses. She printed the date at the top of the page and started to write:

Dear T.S.:

I'm not sure where to begin. These last few days have been extraordinary. I won't presume to know what you must be going through. I'm worried that you are lonely. I'm worried that you are frightened. I'm worried that you are cold. I'm worried that you are being mistreated. I am worried that you may be worried about me.

The day that you called me with the awful news I was having a right good day. I know you'll think me a fool, but I had been to a counselor – yes, I can see your face now, a counselor. I wanted to talk with someone who would just sit and listen to me. Things like how I got to where I am, how we got to where we are; I talked to him about all of that and it felt good, T.S., and it felt good. I suppose I wanted to let things out and then get some perspective or direction. The bottom line, T.S., is that the day you called was the first day in a long while that I had a little spark back into me, a spark that I wanted to use to light a fire with you, to get us back to a healthy, wholesome relationship. You know what I mean love? I had hope.

Then the phone rang. It was you from jail and our entire world was turned upside down.

I thought I didn't love you anymore for a little while there. I thought we had strayed too far off course. Maybe we had and maybe it was too late. I don't think so anymore. I know I love you. I think you love me. I think we have a deep bond lying beneath the surface. But on the surface we have a mundane, unromantic, platonic, dysfunctional existence. All that must change when it can. When can it, T.S.?

I hope you don't find this morose, love. We Englishmen have a way of making everything sound dour. It's not, and I don't mean it to sound that way. I wish I could express myself better, but I'm actually coming 'round to your idea that we can really use this as a wakeup call.

That gets me to an important point, love. I know you don't want to endure the stigma of an insanity plea. Your pride and integrity are positive notions that come from your strong, independent self-reflection. I understand that you are digging your heels in, that you are about to take a hard stand on principle, and that you might end up in prison for far too long. In this very short life, that wouldn't give us any chance to make any go of it. Do you hear me, love?

I talked to Mary, who has been an unbelievable help through all of this, for a long time about your chances if you try for an insanity defense. It's not at all what you think. Some of it is based on impulse, momentary lapses brought about by inner demons. You and I have inner demons, love, our addictions to the games of chance that allow us to avoid realities and responsibilities. You have alluded to it time and again, and if you reflect on it you will see that you succumbed to an inner demon when you hit that poor man. He was the victim of your gambling dependency, your inability to separate right from wrong when it came to the irrational needs driven by the addiction.

Has our pride prevented us from getting help before? We both know it has. Don't let's let it happen again.

There is no way to undo what has been done. The

other bloke is dead. His family will grieve and suffer longstanding loss whether you rot in jail or not. He will remain under the ground whether you are adjudged sane or insane. His kids will hate you whether you're alive or dead. No one will ever understand or forgive you for what happened, whether you take it upon yourself to be a martyr or not. Do you see love? It just is what it is.

I am begging you. Take your best shot to be free as soon as possible. I'm telling you, without reservation, that if you do that I will wait for as long as it takes to give our lives another honest chance.

But love, if you decide to stand on pride and principle and refuse what is the only chance to get back to me soon, then I will move on. I will take your decision to be selfish. I will hold you in disdain and the highest disregard, for having shunned our one and only real chance for happiness together, as incongruous a notion as that may seem in the dire straits in which we find ourselves.

I am past persuasion. I am steadfast. I am yours if you decide now to fight for yourself, to fight for us. What's done is done; what's to come is full of possibility.

I have not said it often, but I say it now without hesitation on the condition that you take your decisions in favor of our love and not against it. Do the right thing now, T.S., please do the right thing now. I love you.

Affectionately,

Edith

She signed her name and put the pen down and folded the paper carefully. She put the letter into her purse and snapped it shut.

She turned up the volume on the TV and pulled the afghan back up around her legs. She watched a show called the "Real Housewives of New York."

"Real housewives, indeed," she thought.

She turned up the volume when sirens from the street outside blared for several minutes. One emergency vehicle after another passed by. Mary came out of the study.

"Holy shit. I never heard such commotion."

"I know. There must've been twenty fire trucks going by."

"It seems to have quieted down now. What have you been doing?"

"Oh, just puttering and watching your vapid American programming. Really, do they make anything other than reality shows?"

"Not so much, these days. It doesn't take much for us to be entertained."

"Apparently not," Edith said and smiled.

Mary went to the kitchen and came back with a chilled bottle of Pinot Gris and two glasses.

"What do you say Edith?"

"Looks good to me."

Mary poured two glasses.

"What were you doing there all hushed up in the study?"

"I was working on a big new case."

"Really," Edith said, "Can you tell me about it or is it all secret under that privilege you guys are always talking about?"

"Normally, I'd say I couldn't tell you about it."

"But in this case you would say yes?"

"Yeah."

"Why's that?"

"Because this case involves your husband."

Edith perked up and leaned forward, "What've you been up to in there?"

"Before or after I decided I wouldn't sit by and watch your husband be a dweeb and give up on his only chance to get out of serious shit?"

"After."

Mary sipped her wine and put her glass down on the coffee table. "OK. I hit the books on what I could do to try to force an insanity defense on T.S."

"How could anyone do something like that? How could you do it?"

"It's tricky. There are some cases that would make it really hard. But it isn't impossible."

Edith took a big gulp of wine. "Be more specific – how would it work?"

"My god, you have been a glutton for punishment

all day with this insanity defense."

"Go on then."

She explained the issues in detail.

"Is it worth a try?" asked Edith.

"You tell me. I'm willing to take a shot at it."

"You're getting more amazing every day."

"I know, I'm a real gem," Mary said, and she filled their glasses.

Mary sat back on the couch and said, "It's getting late. How about we just finish this wine and watch a little TV. Tomorrow is another incredibly busy day."

Edith smiled at Mary with sincere appreciation and admiration. She felt a fondness for Mary that she had felt rarely in her life.

Edith turned the volume back up.

A "Breaking News" bulletin interrupted the broadcast.

The news anchor tried to look very glum.

"There has been an explosion downtown tonight

near the county jail. This just breaking from our on the scene reporters. Initial indications are that gas leaking from a construction site downtown has ignited and exploded violently, creating a pillar of fire over 30 feet high. The source of the ignition is under investigation. Reports of fatalities and injuries are being confirmed and we will bring you the latest as soon as we have more information. Please stay tuned here for more on this breaking story. We will have Sky 11 over the scene shortly."

Mary and Edith looked at each other in disbelief.

"Oh my god, Mary," she screamed. "They said the explosion was near the jail."

"That must've been all the commotion with the fire trucks a little while ago. Shit, how do we find out more," and she was already booting up her laptop. "Let me get a connection and see what I can find out."

"Oh my god," Edith sobbed. "Oh, my god."

"Here is something," Mary said. "Let's see…"

She read the headline from CNN online, "12 dead, 8 missing and at least 33 injured in downtown Las Vegas gas explosion."

"Oh my god. Shit."

"Let's get down there," Edith said.

"Whoa, wait a second. We'll never get close to something like this. Let's think."

Mary picked up her phone and called Bob Scotti. Edith could tell that Mary had reached voice mail. "Bob, this is Mary Roys. Edith and I just saw the news about the gas explosion near the jail and we were hoping you had some information. Please call me as soon as you can. Thanks."

"Fuck it, let's go," Mary said.

They ran out the door toward the car.

When Mary turned onto the street where the county jail was located they were both stunned by the flashing lights of emergency vehicles for as far as the eye could see. They got within two blocks of the jail when they ran into the first police barricade. Mary jumped out of the car and ran up to one of the officers standing behind the barricade.

"Officer, please," she said. "My friend's husband is in county, are you letting anybody through to check on loved ones?"

"Ma'am, I'm sorry," she said, "but this is absolutely off limits to everybody except for first responders. This is still a very unstable and dangerous area."

"But….."

"There are no buts, ma'am. Sorry. I hope you understand."

Of course she did. She walked back to the car.

"Edith, sweetheart, there's no way we're getting close to the jail tonight. Let's go back home and make some calls to try to get more information."

Edith looked at the lights, the smoke, and the flickering flames of hot spots not yet fully extinguished and nodded. The flashing red lights reflected off of her face. Mary turned the car around and they headed back to her house.

Mary's phone rang.

"Hello, Bob, is that you?"

"Yeah, Mary, it's me. I just picked up your call and I'm trying to find out what happened. I was out and not near a TV."

"We just got turned back about two blocks from

the jail. We couldn't tell with all the activity whether the jailhouse was directly involved or not. Do you know anything about that?"

"I don't know anything yet Mary. But I'll do my best to find out. I have more than one client in there tonight."

"I know, Bob. Thanks for any help you can give us."

"Bye."

Edith asked for an update with her eyes.

"He doesn't know anything yet but he's our best chance for finding out. He'll call when he knows something."

It was 12:25 on Tuesday morning when they walked back into the living room of Mary's place and put the TV back on. Mary set her phone next to her, put her laptop on the coffee table and started to search, and they both watched the local network channels for updates.

At 3:12 a.m. Mary's phone rang. She and Edith were half asleep but the ring woke both of them up right away.

"Mary, it's Bob."

"Yes, Bob, what do you know?"

"The explosion tore through at least half of the jail."

"Oh my god," she said. Listening to her response, Edith started to cry.

"What else, Bob?"

"At least eight inmates have been found dead. Your guy is not in that group."

"Thank god," she said. Edith felt hope and moved closer, trying to hear the voice on the other end.

"The Sheriff's office is doing a head count now for the rest. All I know is that most inmates are accounted for."

"What about T.S.?"

"T.S. is missing and unaccounted for, Mary. That's all I know and it's really early in a really chaotic situation so don't jump to any conclusions one way or the other, ok?"

"Yeah, ok. When do you expect to get an update?"

"I'll probably hear again about daybreak. They

expect to have more information for families by mid-morning. I'll keep you updated every time I get any news. Try to get some rest. Tomorrow will be a long day for all of us."

"Yeah, thanks Bob. Good night."

Edith was bursting. "What did he say, Mary?"

"Sit down, Edith," she said, gently pushing her down by the shoulders.

"Mary, please," she begged, "what did he say?"

"They can't find T.S. just yet."

"What do you mean Mary? Is he alright?"

"Honey, no one knows yet. It's crazy down there. You saw it. They'll have more news when it gets light."

"Was the jail damaged?"

"It sounds like part was damaged, but not all. I'm sure it's bedlam everywhere in the area and the sheriff's office is trying to account for everyone now."

"Did anyone at the jail get hurt?"

"There are a few who were killed there Edith,"

and Mary put her arms around Edith.

Edith held Mary tightly and buried her head on Mary's shoulder. Edith started to sob and cry very hard. Mary's tears fell quietly.

Chapter 29

The phone rang at 5:54 on Tuesday morning.

Mary picked it up. She put her hand over the mouthpiece and said "It's Bob," to Edith.

"So, you want us both down there at 7:30?"

She was listening to the voice on the other end.

"OK. Thanks so much," and she hung up. She turned to Edith.

"still no news on T.S. but they've set up a command center across the street from the jail in the Liptak Building. Bob wants us to meet him there at 7:30. They have it set up to provide information to people with family in the jail."

"Do they know anything more," Edith asked.

"Only confirmation of the number dead and confirmation of their identities. The good news is that T.S. is definitely not on that list. They have it down to 3 inmates missing, and T.S. is one of the three."

"This is all so unreal. I'm not sure I can take any more." She paused and collected herself. "I'm going to jump in the shower Mary, is it ok?"

"Sure, Edith. Go ahead. I'll put some water on for tea. Let's get going."

Edith let the hot water run over her head and down her back. She arched her head back and felt the clean rinse over her face and mouth. She breathed in the hot mist to moisten her nostrils, which had dried badly in the Nevada air. She closed her eyes and thought of her home, where it was wet and damp and grey and foggy and oh so lovely. She longed for winding the clock back a week. She wanted a do over so badly she could taste it in the water that slid over her lips. She felt warm and safe in the shower. She let the water pour over her and pour over her and pour over her.

"Edith," she heard Mary yell. "Hurry up, it's almost 6:30."

"Coming, Mary," Edith shouted back, rinsing the shampoo out of her dirty blonde hair. "Sorry!"

"No mind, let's just get a move on."

They took their tea in to go cups and headed back for the jail.

The streets were still cluttered with emergency vehicles and now even more news trucks, many of which were from the national cable networks. Mary was very helpful in navigating through the layers of police security, showing the officers her bar card and explaining the relationship of her companion to one of the missing inmates.

"Good thing we came early, Mary," Edith said while they made their way through the madness. "This is a circus."

"Pretty crazy," Mary said, "but we're almost there."

It was 7:25 when they walked into the lobby of the Liptak Building. The scene inside mirrored the chaos outside. Mary strained her neck to look for Bob Scotti. He was nowhere to be seen among the crowds and clusters of people wandering from here to there and back again. She reached for her cell to send him a text. Within a few seconds he returned the message, "Behind the desk marked Press." She looked around again and saw the Press desk and grabbed Edith's arm to take her in the right direction.

They walked quickly behind the desk and saw Bob talking with an elderly Hispanic couple. The woman was crying and the man was holding his arm firmly around her waist. It looked like she would fall over if he let her go. They knew to wait back until Bob was free. He spotted them out of the corner of his eye and sent the signal that he knew they were there. He spoke for a few more minutes with the couple, hugged the lady and patted the man on the back with a gentle rub, and walked away from them.

"They lost their son," Bob said. "In jail one night for a DUI on his 21st birthday. What a fucking shame."

They could see he was shaken.

"Sorry," he said.

"No problem, Mr. Scotti," Edith said. "What a shame for them."

"Yeah." He cleared his throat and took a breath. "As for T.S. I am afraid there's no new information. They still won't let anyone inside the jail until they finish all of their structural integrity tests and make sure no more gas is leaking anywhere. I have this number," and he handed them both cards, "that you can call 24, 7 for information. It's only for the families of the deceased and the missing. I shouldn't have given it to you Mary, but under…."

She interrupted him. "Thanks, Bob. Don't worry, it goes nowhere."

"I know. Anyway, we can go out into the street if you want to see the jail for yourselves, but that is entirely up to you. There will be a briefing for family at 8:30, so we have until then if you want to go out and take a look."

Mary and Bob looked at Edith. She did not hesitate.

"I want to see."

All three headed for the front revolving door. The street was mostly empty except for a few news camera crews and police, fire and EMS personnel milling around. Mary, Edith and Bob moved to the middle of the street and walked up to the yellow police tape that split the street in two, right down the middle line.

"What an ugly building," Edith said.

The Clark County jail was built in 1958 and had the lack of architectural inspiration coincident with that period in American architecture. It was plain and made of concrete and steel. From the corner there was a concrete block structure with two stories and set back from it was a higher rise steel structure with an additional five floors. It was an odd configuration. The side of the building facing the street was pale blue in the sunlight and did not have any windows. This morning there was a gaping hole in that part of the building, with steel and concrete shards pointing straight out over the street in a starburst created by what must have been a very powerful blast. From the front of the building the three could not see the unsightly HVAC system, but when they walked to the side and around to the back they could. From this vantage point, they could see what looked like a huge white tube climbing the back face of the building and curling up and over top and into what looked like a huge air conditioning unit on the roof. The corner of the concrete block building in the back corner of the building also was badly damaged. The white tube had cracked and opened in several places from top to bottom. There was a white dusty mist gleaming in the sun around the tube. They saw that almost every one of the windows on the third to fifth floors was completely blown out, and huge pieces of deadly glass were strewn on the street around the building. The iron bars that covered the windows were bent and melted in places. The windows on the top two floors were hit and miss – some were blown out and some appeared to be intact. Over the whole of the building there were signs of fire and heat damage.

"T.S. was on the fourth floor," Bob said. "That is if he was in his cell when it happened. All three of the missing are from the same general area."

"What are they doing to search?"

"The police SWAT team is in there now, searching floor to floor and cell block by cell block. They are working very closely, and unfortunately very slowly, with the gas company inspectors who have to secure and clear each sector of the building before it can be searched."

A voice over a bullhorn pierced the morning air and interrupted their discussion.

"Attention! Attention in the building. For those who may be trapped in the building, hear this. Please stay in place. There are search efforts going on now from floor to floor. There are dangerous conditions in the building. Do not move around. Do not light any matches or use any other lighting or ignition sources. Do not kick up any dust. Cover your mouth with a handkerchief or piece of clothing. Do not shout for help unless absolutely necessary. Shouting can cause you to inhale and swallow dangerous amounts of dust. Stay in place.

Help is on the way. I repeat…"

And the message was repeated one more time over the bullhorn.

Mary asked Bob, "Do you know where they are in the search now, Bob. I mean like what floor, what area?"

"No, but I hope we get that information at the briefing at 8:30."

Edith stared at the building and the bright light shining off of the blue façade that faced east. The torn building glowed in the morning sunlight.

"Let's go back inside Edith," Mary said. "We'll find out more there than out here."

"I have to go see about some other families, guys," Bob said, "but I'll look for you inside when they start providing the information. Hang in there," he said.

"We don't have much choice do we, Bob?" Edith said, trying sincerely to be grateful and upbeat.

He smiled and nodded and appreciated her stoicism in the face of such stressful conditions and long odds.

It was 8:43 when the SWAT team commander approached the podium:

"Good morning, everyone. My name is Captain Wade Peterson. I am in charge of the ongoing search and rescue mission in the county jail building across the street. I know that you are here because you have a family member who was in the jail when the explosion occurred. Thankfully, most of you know that your loved one has been accounted for and you know the status of their current conditions. Unfortunately, we do have fatalities and others missing. For the families who have lost a loved one, we are deeply sorry. There are counselors available here to help you and we have information about that in this blue packet on the desk to my right. For those of you with a loved one who has not been accounted for I want to assure you that the Las Vegas police department, in conjunction with the Sheriff's office, the Fire Department, and federal officials, is doing everything possible to safely and quickly find them. We will provide updated reports at a minimum of every four hours and more frequently if circumstances warrant.

Here is what I can tell you right now. A gas leak that started in the construction site just to the west of the jail building was ignited with an unknown ignition source at approximately 10:05 last night. The source of the ignition is under investigation and there is no indication at this point that foul play was involved. There were multiple blasts. One occurred in the eastern most portion of the fourth floor of the building, one occurred near the center rear of the building just below the HVAC unit, and another occurred on the ground floor where the concrete block portion of the building is seamed to the steel structure. We are not sure right now whether there were more than the three blasts we have been able to identify up to now. First responders were on the scene within seven minutes. There were life flight helicopters deployed to take the most serious burn victims to the UNLV Medical Center burn unit. There were fourteen life flight trips between the time of the initial response and midnight. Mobile treatment facilities were established at a safe distance from the blast perimeter to treat the less seriously injured.

Efforts to get a full headcount for inmates and staff started just before 11:00 p.m. By 11:55 we had accounted for all but 33 of the inmates and staff. As of right now we have accounted for all but 3. The search effort for the 3 inmates who are still missing is on the second floor of the front of the building right now. At the present pace, it is taking approximately 4 hours to secure, seal and search one quadrant of one floor. We hope and expect that the pace will quicken over time as the officials from the gas company become more comfortable with the stability of the conditions in and around the building.

We have reason to believe that there are sections of the building that still remain largely intact and that there is sufficient space and oxygen and other means to allow those who are missing to survive for a considerable period of time. But there has been significant and substantial damage to the interior of the building that is not readily apparent from the view from the street. We are optimistic, but our optimism is cautious given the severity of the blast and the amount of damage to the building on the interior.

Many in the media have asked if we have heard any voices or any tapping or other sounds of survivors in the building. To the best of my knowledge, we have not heard anything like that so far. We will let you know if and when we do.

We will be holding a press conference, at which time I will entertain questions from the media after I deliver a statement with an update on the information available. You are all invited to attend that press conference. It will be held right here at 10:00.

I know you all have questions but I also know you understand that I have to get back to work on the mission at hand, and I beg your pardon for excusing myself now to do that. Thank you."

And as various voices yelled questions, the Captain hurried off from behind the podium and the microphone and disappeared into a hallway behind the place where he spoke to the anxious crowd.

"Let's find a place to sit and wait until the next update," Mary said.

Edith did not respond. She followed Mary to a row of folding chairs lined up against the far wall and facing onto the street. They sat. And they waited.

Edith fumbled through her purse looking for a scrap of paper that she had shoved into her bag as they were heading out the door. She pulled out the crumpled sheet and smoothed out the wrinkles as best as she could. She stared down at the words, which T.S. had handwritten for his poetry class during the last year of university:

"In the end it will be the end,

I know not what awaits there.

Until the end I will fear the end,

Not knowing what awaits there.

There are those who say there are those who know,

I know not on what they base it.

It seems to me that in the end

It only helps them face it."

She dried her eyes with the pale blue tissue she was clutching in her right hand. She wiped the moisture from beneath her nose and threw the tissue in the waste basket on the floor. She gazed out the window at the steel and concrete edifice with the huge hole in its midsection.

Mary and Edith both saw Bob Scotti at the same time. He walked quickly toward them, with papers in his right hand. They stood up. Edith stumbled as she struggled to maintain her balance.

Bob moved directly to Edith. "They found him, Edith."

Bob looked at Mary and then back at Edith and he finally said, "I am so sorry, Edith. They found him dead."

Edith put her hand over her mouth, which was wide open but no sound was coming out. Mary put both of her arms around Edith and held her close. Bob stepped back and hung his head.

After a short while, Edith looked up at Bob and said, "How?"

"They aren't sure, and I'm afraid they won't be sure until they finish an autopsy. Off the record they say it looks like some kind of blunt trauma, like something hit him in the front of his neck, in the throat."

"Oh, my god," Edith said and she looked quite ill. Mary moved in immediately to comfort her. Edith backed away. Bob interjected with a sense of some urgency.

"Maybe it's best if I let the medical examiner explain Edith. I don't want to get anything wrong…"

Mary put her hand up to signal for Bob to stop talking.

"I'll leave the two of you alone," he said, "I'm so

sorry." He backed up and turned and walked back out onto the street.

Edith tried to pull herself together. Mary waited and comforted her patiently.

"What now, Mary? I have no bloody idea what to do now?"

"I don't either Edith. But let me take care of figuring that out," Mary said. "I'll find out from the medical examiner's office what happens next and I'll help you through all of it. I am so sorry Edith, so very sorry." Mary's heart was truly broken. Maybe for the first time, for real.

"I know you are, Mary. I truly do."

Edith sat back down and looked at the hole in the building across the street. It matched the one in her heart. She started to hum and bounce her leg up and down like she had done in awkward situations when she was a little girl.

"Will you be alright for just a minute, Edith?" Mary asked her, placing a soft hand on her shoulder.

"Yes, quite alright Mary. I will be alright for a little awhile. But try not to be long."

"OK. I won't be long. I'm going to go and talk with the authorities and see what needs to be done." She turned to walk away and as if she had forgotten her purse she turned quickly and said to Edith, "You don't want to come do you?"

Edith looked up, a bit startled because she thought Mary had gone. "No, Mary. If you're willing to deal with it I'd be ever so grateful. Ever so indeed."

Mary nodded. "I just wanted to make sure you were comfortable with me going ahead. You stay put and I'll take care of it."

Mary bent down and stroked Edith's hair gently on each side of her head and then walked out and away toward the incident command center. Edith resumed humming. Her foot started to tap, rhythmically.

Chapter 30

News of the death of T.S. Fowler arrived in Northern Kentucky. By Friday it was common knowledge everywhere in the town, and rumors spread like a wildfire.

Very early on Sunday morning, Jimmy Gatlin woke up in a cold sweat. He looked at the clock. It was only 3:45 a.m. He could not sleep. He was still a bit drunk from the night before. He pulled on his undershorts and stepped out of bed. He walked into the kitchen and pulled the half empty mason jar from the refrigerator and took a big gulp of the Kentucky white lightning. He put the top back on the jar and carried it onto the back porch.

Jimmy took the handgun and put it on the rotting picnic table. He sat in the broken down rocking chair and screwed the top from the jar and took another swig. He put the jar down and reached into his shirt pocket. He pulled out a clip for the handgun and slowly slapped it into place. Now fully loaded, he set the gun back down and stared at the barrel. Then he looked up at the stars in the sky. He folded his arms over his chest and dozed off. The sun woke him up a few hours after.

Sunday morning was usually slow and easy in the

small Kentucky town where Mrs. Dan Berry was trying to resume her life. Hung-over men got dressed to go to church, with pounding headaches they hid from their wives. At the same time doting housewives and mothers cleaned up their kids to show them off, good manners and all. Mrs. Dan Berry was solo. She did not have children, not yet anyway. And she no longer had a husband. She sat alone in the fourth pew in the small Baptist church where she had worshiped with Dan each Sunday morning for years. This time, and from now on, she would listen to the Reverend without Dan by her side.

A cool breeze blew through the open door at the back of the church. Jimmy Gatlin sat where he could feel the breeze. It was helping him stay awake. He felt uneasy because he had a handgun in his coat pocket, and he had forgotten to put on the safety before he sat down in the pew. Now, he was too nervous to do anything but sit as quietly as possible.

It was comfortable inside and no one needed to use the paper bulletin for a fan. The choir was sitting down, out of breath from a rousing rendition of *Amazing Grace*. There was a low sound of stirring while the congregation quieted and settled in on the rough wooden benches for the

Reverend's talk. In a short while all seemed still. The ceiling fan whirred quietly, and the cool breeze stirred amongst them all. A speck of sweat was moving slowly down Jimmy Gatlin's nose. He stayed perfectly still and it fell harmlessly onto the floor between his feet.

Breaking the silence, with a booming voice, the Reverend said, "Just about a week ago we sent our dear brother Dan Berry to his eternal resting place. God bless and rest his weary soul, amen. We, as a Christian community and extended family, mourned a loss. And at the same blessed and sacred time, amen, we celebrated a life. We came together right here," and he pointed with great emphasis at his feet, "right here where we gather again today on this glorious Sunday morning. And when we were together then, brothers and sisters, we asked why?" He looked with an impassioned plea toward the heavens for dramatic emphasis. He yelled out with arms outstretched toward the sky, "And we cried out to god almighty – why? In the name of your son Jesus Christ, amen, why?"

All was still. The ceiling fan whirred. The Reverend knew how to milk a moment. He did.

After what he deemed the appropriate time, the Reverend looked down toward Mrs. Berry, and when he caught her eye he moved on.

"And we searched for an answer. We prayed and sang our praise in search of an answer. And when all was said and done and sung, there is and was only one answer – that god knows best. Can I get an amen from you this morning?" and the congregation gave an amen.

He closed his eyes and opened them just before he continued, "God works in such mysterious ways, brothers and sisters, in such great and oh so mysterious ways. We, as mere men, cannot divine his sacred intention or plan. That is his gift. The gift of love and fate and destiny."

Jimmy Gatlin stirred ever so slightly and put a soft hand on the lump in his coat pocket.

The Reverend pushed back from the pulpit. He took the microphone from the stand and pulled the cord around to give him the freedom to walk among his flock.

Standing in the middle of the congregation, with his back toward Mrs. Berry, he went on toward the climax, "But we resolved then," he paused, "and we reconfirm today," he paused, "our commitment in faith," he paused, "Hallelujah Jesus," he paused, "that only god knows why brother Dan," he paused and took a huge inward breath, "was taken when he was taken." He paused for a longer time. "We were," he paused, "we are," he paused, "and we will remain," he paused and fell to his knees, whispering into the microphone, "at peace with that."

There was a hush. After what seemed like an eternity, he rose to his feet. He was now talking almost in tongues, in an out of body experience, "In all things, even in such as these, there is a will, a purpose, and a way."

The congregation listened and fidgeted. Mrs. Berry sat alone and very still. The Reverend seemed to reconnect with his surroundings and he walked back to the pulpit and replaced the microphone into its stand.

Jimmy Gatlin was feeling dizzy. His right hand started to shake ever so slightly as it felt the gun on the other side of the fabric.

The Reverend went on, "And as we came to understand and embrace the mysteries of the almighty father's actions, we struggled with what to feel, how to feel, about the man whose act brought brother Dan to his end. What justice would be right? Who should hand it out? How should we proceed with our thoughts regarding the trial, the conviction and the punishment of the man who took our friend and brother's life?"

The Reverend loosened his collar and sipped from a glass of water. He pulled the microphone closer to his mouth, and he spoke softer and in a deeper tone for emphasis.

"I heard the talk in town," he paused. "I heard and felt the venom," he paused, "and the anger," he paused, "and the hard and strong appetite for retribution." He looked out with disdain over his flock. "I saw the angry faces in the barber shop. God bless." He paused. "I felt the fire of the hatred in the grocery store. God bless." He paused. "I sensed the power of evil," he paused, "the power of evil itself taking over good men and women, god fearing and god loving men and women." He paused and gave the impression that his stomach hurt. "And it pained me to my core." He looked down at his bible and he smiled and picked it up and held it close to his breast. "I prayed on it friends. I prayed on it hard. And the answer came to me as softly and easily as a summer rain," he paused and said almost imperceptibly, "men are not worthy to judge. Men are not worthy to punish."

The Reverend paused for a deep breath.

He then said, as if a matter of fact, "The man who took it upon himself, for the love of money, for the greed that corrupts us all, to end the life of our dear brother ultimately has one judge, just as we do. For reasons we will not know, just as we know them not for brother Dan, the man who killed our friend met his ultimate fate just days ago. He was sitting in wait to be judged, waiting for men to decide his fate. But god intervened and took the decision out of man's hands."

Mrs. Berry perspired. Jimmy Gatlin felt sick to his stomach and feared that he would throw up right there and then.

"So do we pray for his soul or do we revel in his demise?" He paused again so his followers could ponder this important point. It was meant as a rhetorical question.

"We pray for him brothers and sisters. We pray for him and for his loved ones left behind. And we thank god for the solution and the resolution and for sparing men the job of judging, convicting and punishing."

A few men in the back of the church shuffled their feet and whispered to each other. Jimmy Gatlin tightened his grip.

"For not one of us is better than another. We are all frail. We are all mired in sin. We are all wholly dependent on the almighty father for grace and heavenly help. And we are all subject to fate, chance and the luck of the draw unless," and he paused with great dramatic flair, "unless we firmly take the reins," he paused, "and follow the guiding light of our lord," he paused and shook his head violently back and forth and to and fro, "to navigate past the wickedness," he paused and shook his head, "the temptation," he paused and shook his head and his fists, "and the vile reality of a godless life."

The Reverend wiped his brow with a wrinkled white handkerchief. He sat back down for a moment as if he would otherwise be swept away. After a few moments, he rose unsteadily. He moved back to the pulpit and grabbed each side for balance and dear life.

"As we worship on Sundays and as we serve the lord every day, let us remember human frailty, let us embrace divine intervention, and let us steer clear of the bad chances that take us off of the path to eternal happiness."

The Reverend sat down, appearing exhausted. The choir took up with "Soon and Very Soon." The plate passed amidst and among the pews as the Reverend appeared to nap, spent and content.

When services were over, the Reverend stood at the back of the church and greeted his congregation one by one as they left. When Mrs. Dan Berry got her turn with the Reverend she looked up and slowly removed the large sunglasses she wore to hide her puffy, bloodshot eyes.

"That was an interesting homily, Reverend."

"Why, thank you, Mrs. Berry. I suspected that of all people you would understand and appreciate it."

"This time, Reverend, you thought wrong. And I wish you had the decency to talk to me before using my name and my dead husband's name and my dreadful situation to make your point," she paused, "a point I don't agree with."

He looked at her with his head cocked ever so slightly and said softly, "I don't understand Mrs. Berry."

She shook her head before she started. "I wanted

that son of a bitch to die by lethal injection. I wanted him to know in advance about the way he was going to die and to be able to think about it, or even better yet, let him struggle with how not to think of it. Just like I struggle every day with trying not to think about how my husband is dead and about how I had no child with him and how I will not have a child without him and about how he had no reason to be killed by some desperate, greedy son of a bitch who loved money more than life. I wanted him to wither slowly counting down the days until his life would be snuffed out. I wanted him to have the desperate hope of appeals and then have them mercilessly denied, the haunting of protestors on the prison lawn, the terror of the fitful nightmare of choosing a last meal. I wanted his wife to suffer long and slow while her husband waited on death row. I wanted vengeance. I wanted satisfaction. I wanted someone else to hurt as badly as I hurt. Your sermon was full of shit, Reverend. Totally full of shit."

Mrs. Berry put her sunglasses back on and walked quickly to the car waiting for her in the front of the church. Several others standing around and who had been listening walked away slowly, turning now and again to shake their heads at the

Reverend.

"You missed a real good opportunity to fire us all up today, preacher," said one gaunt man while he walked away, "missed a real good opportunity for sure." He spit some chew onto the church lawn. "Damn, could have been some real fire and brimstone today." He spit again and adjusted the wad in his mouth with his right index finger, "Hot damn, shoulda been some good down home shit today for sure."

The Reverend stood alone at the bottom step to the front entrance of the church. The parking lot was empty and the cool breeze blew past and over him.

As the Reverend went into the church, he did not notice one car left alone in the parking lot. Inside the car, Jimmy Gatlin was taking a sip of moonshine with his left hand and holding a handgun so tightly in his right that his knuckles were white.

Chapter 31

The jumbo jet landed at Heathrow. Edith jerked forward in her seat when the wheels touched down hard and the impact jolted her awake. A little more than a week earlier she had taken off for Las Vegas to help her husband in trouble. She was returning a widow.

The Brit did not have life insurance. Edith could not afford to fly his body back to England. She buried him in a small public cemetery in Las Vegas. She thought it oddly fitting. It was very simple and very plain and very frugal. It had to be.

Edith went to the station where the Heathrow Express would carry her and her possessions to Paddington Station in London. She chose the quiet car, where cell phones and other audio devices were not permitted. Quiet was what she wanted and what she needed.

The train pulled away from the station right on time.

She gazed out of the window, watching first as the pillars of the underground station whisked by faster and faster until they formed a picket fence before her eyes. Then suddenly the train emerged and the lights from the airport and surrounding roads and traffic filled the view. She settled in and focused now on the soft lights of the interior of the train.

What a nightmare the last 10 days had been. It seemed years ago that she had talked with Lunat, the therapist. It seemed like a different time altogether when she had strolled on that sunny day afterward and enjoyed a pub lunch and a rest by the river. From that point forward, it seemed like a lifetime had come and gone.

Edith turned on her cell phone for the first time she had switched it off at JFK in New York. There was a message light flashing and she clicked on the envelope icon. She had a text from Mary.

"Hope this finds you safe and sound back in London. Miss you already. I'm here if you need anything. Best, Mary."

What an angel, Edith thought. What would I have done without her? How will I ever repay her?

She scrolled down to the next message, another from Mary: "News from the M.E.'s office. The autopsy report is available. Do you want to see it? Call when you can. Mary."

Shit, Edith thought. Do I want to read something that macabre? Not really, she thought. But then again she needed to know and she needed to be able to explain to the Brit's parents, who were beside themselves with grief and guilt, with no second chance for any reconciliation with their son. Not now.

She started to text back to Mary: "Made it back safely. On train now to city. Thanks again for everything. You're a living doll. About the autopsy," she waited a moment and then continued, "as much as I'll regret it, please send it along by email if you can. I suppose I need to know, as painful as it might be." She took a moment before finishing with, "Can't wait to talk with you. Will call soon. Edith."

She read the message and then hit the send button.

Edith got home and went to her computer. The email with the PDF attachment was in Edith's inbox. She clicked on it and waited for it to open. She started to read the report. Wow, that was quick, she thought, and she glanced at her watch to see what time Mary had sent the message from Las Vegas.

She skipped through the preliminary paragraphs. She skimmed to look for the cause of death. Her eyes focused on the words in all capital letters:

"BLUNT LARYNGEAL TRAUMA."

Edith was confused with the technical format. She pushed on.

"Anatomical Summary:

1. Blunt force trauma to neck.

2. Hyoid bone fractures and epiglottic injuries causing airway obstruction.

3. Displaced or angulated thyroid cartilage fracture.

4. Asphyxiation."

She read through complicated notes and procedures. She found another underlined portion that discussed the cause of death: "Cause of death of this thirty-three year old male is blunt force trauma to the larynx and associated areas, subsequently causing asphyxiation."

She read the paragraph that described how her dead husband had been found:

"The body was first seen by me after I was called to the Clark County jail following what was alleged to have been a gas explosion in or near the building the night before. I arrived at the jail at approximately 8:45 a.m. and entered the room where the decedent's body was found and located. I made a preliminary assessment and viewed the body as it sat somewhat upright on a desk chair behind a desk. The police had covered the body with a sheet. On removing the sheet from the body, the decedent was found to be sitting with his arms straight down to his sides. The head was bent slightly forward. A quick and preliminary examination of the body revealed multiple lacerations. In addition there was extensive damage to the throat and neck areas. There was significant blood spatter around the room."

Edith pulled back from the computer and took a breath. She stood and walked slowly to the kitchen and pulled a bottle of water out of the fridge. She opened the bottle and took a large gulp. She bent over and leaned on the counter until she regained her wits. She put the cap back on the bottle and took it with her back into the living room. She sat back down, put the bottle on the stand next to the table and continued to read. There was graphic detail on the external exam. The final line mentioned the wedding band she had slipped on the Brit's finger on their wedding day.

Edith sobbed uncontrollably. She eventually was able to dismiss the image of the wedding band on her husband's lifeless finger, and she was able to read on.

Edith paused as she caught a glimpse of the next section of the report: "Internal Exam." She took a sip from the water bottle but it was empty. She stood slowly and walked back into the kitchen. She threw away the empty bottle and opened the refrigerator door. She pulled out another bottle of water and then replaced it. She grabbed a bottle of beer. She reached into the drawer and shuffled around for the bottle opener. She found it, lifted it out, and opened the beer. She took a long drink, throwing her head back and swallowing deeply. She went back to the living room and sat down to read the rest.

"Internal Exam:

1. The body was opened with a Y-shaped thoracoabdominal incision."

Edith sat back to catch her breath. The image was overwhelming. She skipped over the descriptions of the organs, their weights, their appearance and conditions. She moved all the way to the very end of the report.

"Opinion:

The decedent sustained a blunt force trauma to the front of the throat/neck area that caused the larynx to be crushed. In addition blunt force trauma caused fractures to the hyboid bone and significant injuries to the epiglottis. These injuries resulted in eventual asphyxiation, which occurred approximately 10 hours after the initial blunt trauma. The remainder of the autopsy revealed a normal, healthy adult male with no congenital anomalies. The only nonfatal observation was the apparent onset of a blood disease as evidenced by abnormalities in the marrow.

Signed electronically,

Dr. Graham Oldham, Deputy Medical Examiner."

Edith was numb. She pushed down the computer screen to hide the report. She tried not to think about the process, but she kept seeing the picture in her head – of sharp knives and bright spot lights and jars of tissues and jars with organs. She saw small scales with a liver on one and a lung on one and a heart on one. She closed her eyes so tightly that they hurt but the visions would not go away. She screamed as loudly as she could. Finally, the visions were gone. She picked up the beer bottle and chugged the rest down. She looked at the clock. It was too early to call Mary.

She felt emptiness in her stomach, but she knew she could not eat.

Chapter 32

Jimmy was in Judge Lanham's courtroom chatting with the court stenographer, waiting for the judge to take the bench. The courtroom was crowded, as usual, with lawyers, defendants, and family and friends and victims. The docket was crowded with arraignments and motions. Jimmy glanced up at the clock.

"Geez," he said to the reporter, "he's really behind time today."

"Yeah, we'll be lucky to finish for a late lunch. You think you should check on him?"

"Yeah, I better. He starts to read the paper and loses all track of time. Let me see what's going on."

Jimmy walked in front of the bench and went through the door that led back to Judge Lanham's chambers. He knocked on the judge's door and did not get an answer. He paused, and then knocked again. Nothing. He went back out into the courtroom.

"Did you see the judge come in this morning?" he asked the bailiff.

"Yeah, he got here around 7:45 and went straight

into his chambers. Why?"

"Because he's late as hell and I can't get any response when I knock on his door."

"Do you want me to come back with you?"

"Yeah, that would be good. This is freaking me out. He always answers when I knock."

They both went back to the judge's chambers and the bailiff knocked loudly and long. They both stepped back and waited.

"What is it?" the judge said at last.

"Jimmy, here, judge. We're way behind schedule. You alright?"

Again, no response.

Jimmy looked at the bailiff. He whispered, "What should we do?"

"Let's go in."

Jimmy opened the door. The judge's robes were hanging in the plastic wrap from the laundry on the coat rack in the far corner of the room. They had not been touched this morning. The judge was facing away from Jimmy and the bailiff, turned toward the back wall in his leather swivel chair.

On the judge's desk was a half empty bottle of Irish whiskey. The judge turned around quickly and faced the two with a half full glass of ice and whiskey in his right hand and a letter opener in his left. He held the opener like a dagger.

"Judge, what's wrong?" Jimmy said and motioned for the bailiff to leave them alone. The bailiff backed up slowly and out of the door, never taking his eyes from the judge.

"What's wrong, Jimmy? Every fucking thing is wrong Jimmy. What fucking thing isn't wrong?"

His words were thick and muddled by the whiskey.

"Judge, you have a courtroom full of cases. What should I do?"

"Whatever the fuck you want Jimmy. That's what I do."

Jimmy moved closer to the judge and sat down. He wasn't sure what to do.

"Do you wanna talk about it?"

"Talk about it? Sure, Jimmy I wanna talk about it. You wanna drink?"

Jimmy shook his head no and the judge filled the glass with more ice and topped it off with whiskey.

"I'll talk about it Jimmy. What's to fucking talk about? The fucking poor bastard's dead."

There was a long pause.

"Who, judge? Who's dead?"

"The poor British bastard. The poor fuck who came in here with a plea bargain. A plea that I didn't approve. Why didn't I approve it Jimmy?"

He waited and Jimmy did not answer.

"Where does the bastard go if I approve it Jimmy?"

The judge waited for an answer.

"I asked you a fucking question!"

"He checks out of county and goes to Graterford."

"Precisely, Jimmy. And where does he go when I piss all over his plea bargain and when I piss all over the DA and when I piss all over the PD? Where does he go then, Jimmy?"

"Back to county, judge."

"Right again, Jimmy, you're a real cracker jack. Right again."

The judge rubbed his eyes hard and shook his glass so the ice would rattle and melt into the brown whiskey.

"Because of my hard on for the English over the fucking Lockerbie bomber. I fucking take it out on this poor guy who has no more to do with any of that than the fucking man on the fucking moon."

He took a long sip of the whiskey and he grimaced.

"And I never even read the motion papers, Jimmy. I still haven't read them. For all I know the guy was innocent. I was just making it up as I went along at the hearing Jimmy."

The judge tried to straighten himself in the chair.

"Do you know how often I do that?"

He drank again before continuing.

"I had to get a fucking hard on for the English just before this sad sack waltzes in here with a deal he thinks is going to be approved. He thinks he'll

334

report to Graterford and start serving his time and start marking the days off of the calendar on the wall. But he doesn't know who's sitting in judgment that day, Jimmy? A bitter, frustrated, warped old Irish judge with a wee bit of a hard on for the English. So I don't approve the deal Jimmy. You remember, right? Sure, I was a real smart ass, a regular tough guy. I played god and sentenced the fucker to death by sending him back to the county jail, which proceeds against all fucking odds to fucking blow up on the guy. And he's not supposed to be there. See, Jimmy, I put him there because I could put him there, with my fucking black robes and big gavel. What a fucking joke, Jimmy."

Jimmy says, "But that's not your fault judge. He was going to jail somewhere."

"That's the point Jimmy," and the judge stood up leaning over the desk with his arms supporting his weight. "That's the point. Fate. I put him where the explosion happened. I put him in harm's way. I made the choice that started the chain of events that led to his death. My wrongheaded decision leads to a wrong result. And it was all meant to be. It was all meant to be derived from that decision. Wrong begets wrong."

The judge was out of breath, so he paused to catch it. He sat back down and his face faded from the bright red it had acquired while he stood.

"And just because of my bitterness, and my frustration, and my fucking demagoguery, the son of a bitch is dead."

He spun his chair toward the wall and away from Jimmy and kept talking. His voice was soft now.

"I never think of them as people anymore. Not as people."

The judge took another drink. He looked Jimmy square in the eyes.

"It's not just this case, Jimmy. This case was just the straw that broke the camel's back. This British guy was one among many. Many more than you could ever imagine, Jimmy."

Lanham burped. He looked embarrassed, like a child who just farted in church. He took a sip and went on.

"They are all like ghosts to me. Like ghosts that come in and go out of my courtroom with no footprint, no mark, no trace of their ever really having been there. It's been that way for years,

Jimmy. Fucking years."

Jimmy was rigid and motionless. The judge was no longer speaking to Jimmy. After a long, deep breath the judge looked up at the ceiling and continued with his soliloquy.

"I don't think about where they've come from. I don't give a fuck about where they will go. I don't think about them at all. I just want them to leave; to leave my courtroom, and to leave me alone."

The judge whirled around and took a sip to empty his glass. He tried to stand up and reach for his robes, but he stumbled back into his seat.

"No court today, judge," Jimmy said. "Just sit back down and I'll cancel the docket and get you some coffee. You can't leave this room in your condition. You hear me, judge? You must stay here until I get back."

The judge nodded. "I wish I had a gun here today, Jimmy. Oh boy, I wish I had a fucking big gun."

Jimmy walked back into the courtroom and shot a glance at the bailiff. The bailiff nodded his head no, which Jimmy took to mean he had not told anyone about the judge's condition. Jimmy nodded back with approval.

"Ladies and gentlemen, the judge isn't well today. The docket is canceled. Please check with the clerk for re-scheduling. If anyone has a time critical issue on a speedy trial, then go see the calendar control judge right now for an emergency re-assignment. I'm closing this room in five minutes, so be quick about getting out. Sorry."

He walked back into the judge's chambers. Judge Lanham had his face buried in his arms flat face forward on his desk. The bottle of Irish whiskey was leaning over onto his right arm. The empty glass was to his left. Jimmy picked up the bottle and the glass and stashed them in the credenza behind the desk. He put a sweater over the judge's shoulders. He locked the door to the chambers with his key and left to go downstairs for some hot, black coffee.

Chapter 33

Mary Roys sat on her porch with a cup of iced coffee in her hand and her cell phone in the other. She was checking voice messages and emails. She heard the doorbell ring.

"Odd," she said out loud.

She got up to go to the door. She tossed the phone onto the couch and put the cup of coffee on the table in front of it.

"Who is it?" she said as she peered through the peephole.

"It's Scotti," she heard the voice come back at her.

She opened the door.

"Bob, what a surprise. Come on in."

"Sorry to drop by without calling first, but it's been kind of crazy and I wanted to make sure I talked to you before I was bombarded with another hundred things to do. This explosion has completely mucked up the criminal docket."

"I can only imagine," she said, and motioned for him to sit down on the couch. "Can I get you something?"

"No, thanks. I can only stay a few minutes."

"OK," she said and she picked up her coffee. "What's up?"

"A couple of things. Did you hear about Lanham?"

"No, I don't keep up much with the criminal court. What happened?"

"Word is he had a bit of a meltdown after the explosion – nobody I talk to seems to know exactly why – and he resigned from the bench."

"That's odd. Why would the explosion upset him that much?"

"Nobody knows. They say he is spending most of his early retirement deep down at the bottom of a whiskey glass."

"A shame, and very odd," she said.

He nodded in agreement.

Bob then said, "I never thought I'd end up feeling sorry for that bastard."

Mary took a sip of coffee.

Bob went on, "Anyway, that's obviously not what

I came to talk to you about."

He reached into his coat pocket and pulled out a soiled business sized envelope. He held it up and waved it gently in front of Mary.

He said, "This is what I came to talk with you about."

"What is it?" she said, surprised by his flair for the dramatic.

Bob put the envelope down on the coffee table just out of Mary's reach.

He went on, "The sheriff's office called me last night right around the end of the day and told me the coroner found this envelope in the back hip pocket of my client's jail jumpsuit."

Mary leaned forward to look more closely at the envelope.

"Really?" she said.

"Yeah, the coroner apparently forgot about it in the confusion after the explosion. Of course, the DA's office read it, so it was opened. They kept a copy because it has some information that they need, but they wouldn't tell me what it was. They gave it to me since they had no one else to give it to."

"Can I see it?" she said.

"Sure," Bob said and he picked it up and handed it to Mary. "But it's resealed and has to stay that way."

She nodded and picked it up. It was dirty and a bit rumpled. It had obviously been opened and then re-sealed. On the front, in neat printed letters it simply said Dear Edith. Mary turned the envelope over and around in her hands several times. She held it up to the light coming from the lamp on the side table. She could see writing, but could not make anything out. All the while, Bob watched her.

"We don't know each other that well, Mary, but I need your help with this. You know my client's wife better than anybody over here. This is going to be quite a surprise for her and maybe even quite a blow. I was hoping you could get in touch with her and get it to her safely and unopened. I think the news would sit better with her if it came from you. And I think she would understand better about why it had been opened if you explained it. Are you ok with that?"

Mary took a sip of her coffee and said, "Sure, Bob.

I'll take care of it."

He stood up and started to walk to the door. She stood up and followed him.

He turned as he put his hand on the knob, "Thanks, Mary. I appreciate it. What a mess."

"You're welcome, Bob."

He smiled, turned the knob to open the door, and walked out. She pulled the door closed behind him and latched it. She watched until he got into his car and then switched off the porch light. She stared out onto the dark street for another minute and then turned to walk back to the table where the envelope laid quietly.

Mary thought for a few minutes about what to do about this and when. It was too late to call Edith now, so she would have time to think things over before they could talk the following day.

Mary picked up the phone and punched in numbers. She put the phone up to her ear.

The voice on the other end was not pleased.

"Mary, Jesus H. Christ. Are you kidding me? I am so pissed. Why haven't' you called me. I left a bunch of messages. Jesus Christ, what the fuck!"

Natalie said without letting Mary get a word in edge wise.

"I know, Natalie. I'm so sorry."

"Jesus Christ," Natalie said, and then she started to calm down. "This better be good, Mary, real goddamned good."

"If by good you mean interesting, it is."

Mary brought Natalie up to speed on everything that had happened since Mary picked up Edith at the Las Vegas airport many days earlier. Her account was interrupted intermittently by Natalie with "No, shit," and "You're fucking kidding me," and "What a shame."

"So why are you calling me now?" Natalie asked.

"Because even though I don't deserve it after how shitty I've been I need some girl advice."

"Fucking A you don't deserve it," Natalie said.

Mary went ahead, "Edith's husband's lawyer came here tonight and gave me a letter that her husband must've written when he was trapped in the jail. He asked me to get in touch with her and get it to her. It would be hard enough to do in person, but

344

how the hell do I do it over the phone?"

There was no immediate reply.

"Natalie? Are you still there?" Mary asked.

"Yeah, just thinking."

Mary waited.

After a short while Natalie spoke again, "I think you just call her and tell her."

"Tell her what?" Mary said, perplexed.

"Just what happened is what you tell her. But be careful about telling her it's a letter to her. You don't know that."

Mary had not considered this, even though she was hard pressed to think of anything else it might be.

Natalie went on, "I mean she's dealing with the fact that he's dead and this is one of many things that a widow deals with after a husband's death. I mean she's over there dealing with bank accounts, and credit cards, and lease papers, and estate documents, and vehicle titles, cleaning out his closet," she stopped talking for a second and then said, "Jesus Christ, Mary, she's dealing with a ton of shit." She stopped again to take a breath. "This'll be another thing to add to all of that other shit. A little weirder maybe, but another in a long list of weird things."

"I guess," Mary said, "but wouldn't this freak you out? Waiting for an envelope that might be your dead husband's final message to you?"

"You're being too dramatic and assuming too many things."

"What am I assuming?" Mary shot back.

"That he knew he was going to die when he wrote this, for one. That it wasn't in his pocket from two days before he died. Anyway, it kinda is what it is and the less of a huge deal you make of it when you tell her about it, the less of a huge deal she'll make about it while she's waiting to get it."

Mary reflected on Natalie's last point.

"I think you're right. I think I just tell her as a matter of fact that there's an envelope for her from her husband and that I'll send it overnight. Does that sound ok?" Mary asked.

"Exactly," Natalie said. "Whether the message is good, bad or indifferent, there's no reason to rile

Edith up if you can help it."

"I like that plan," Mary said.

"Me too," Natalie said.

"And listen, please forgive me for not calling you back. If I had a good excuse I'd use it. I don't. I just kinda got really involved with Edith and the whole thing and didn't focus on anything else for a few days. I'm really sorry."

"I'll get over it," Natalie said.

"Well how about we get over it together over lunch sometime next week?"

"That sounds good, why don't you call me and we will pick a day," Natalie said.

"Let's pick a day now, my track record on calling you isn't that good."

"Fair enough. Let me look real quick here at my calendar."

There was a pause while Natalie looked at her schedule and Mary was doing the same.

"How about Tuesday at 12:30?" Natalie said.

"Works for me. Let's do it," Mary said, relieved

that her inconsideration had not ruined a burgeoning friendship. "And thanks again for your help, and for not staying really pissed at me."

"Let's see how lunch goes. You're not out of the woods yet."

"OK, Natalie. Ok. I'll see you next week."

"OK, bye," Natalie said.

"Bye," Mary said.

Mary took the envelope and placed it in the top drawer of her office desk.

The next morning Mary got up early. She hadn't slept well, going over her upcoming phone conversation with Edith over and over and over.

It was time to make the call.

Mary picked up the phone and dialed the country code for England and followed with the phone number for Edith's mobile phone. It seemed like the phone rang forever.

Finally, "Hello?"

"Edith, Mary here in Las Vegas. How are you?"

"Mary, how lovely to hear from you. I'm fine, I

guess. As fine as one might reasonably expect. How are you?" Edith said, genuinely excited to hear her new friend's voice.

"I'm good, Edith, good. Listen I called for more than to just say hello."

"Yes, what is it Mary?" Edith said, becoming a little concerned.

"It is nothing at all to worry about Edith," and she pushed on, "they just found an envelope from T.S that looks like it's for you and they asked me to get in touch with you and to get it to you. So I will send it straight away, ok?"

There was no sound coming from the other end. Mary waited for a few seconds.

"Edith, honey, are you still there?" Mary asked, in what she tried to make a soothing voice.

"Yes, I'm here. Just a bit taken aback. Where did they find it?"

"In his pocket Edith. They found it in his pocket and Mr. Scotti brought it to me last night. It was too late to call you then so I decided to wait until this morning," Mary said, trying to follow the advice from Natalie to be as matter of fact about the whole thing as possible.

"In his pocket when he died?" Edith asked.

This is not going well, Mary thought.

"I suppose so Edith."

"How perfectly dreadful. Is it opened? What can you tell me about it?"

"It was opened by the district attorney's office. That's standard Edith; they read all mail to and from the inmates. But they re-sealed it."

"Oh my, Mary. Oh my, indeed. What could it be?"

Mary said honestly, "I don't know Edith. But until I get it to you neither of us will know. Can I send it by overnight courier?"

Edith answered in a voice that was quivering, "Yes, Mary. Please do. You have the address right?" Edith said, and they confirmed the address was right.

Mary said, "Please promise me you won't worry about this Edith. Please?"

"I'll try Mary, but my stomach is in a knot and my heart is pounding. Just send it the fastest way. Will you? I will pay you for the shipping."

"I will," Mary said, "and don't be silly about the shipping."

"Thank you so much Mary. I'll call you to let you know I get it Mary. Thank you so very much for everything you have done, including this."

"You're welcome," Mary said, and when there was no reply she said, "You know, it's funny but I really miss you."

"Not funny at all Mary. I miss you too."

Mary felt tears welling up and decided the call should end before she ended up breaking down.

"I'll wait to hear from you Edith. Take care," she said, holding back more serious tears.

"I will, Mary. You too."

Mary put the phone down and sobbed. Edith put the phone in her pocket and stared into space, deeply absorbed in thought.

Chapter 34

The phone rang on the other end and Edith anxiously waited for an answer.

"Good day, Ivan Lunat's office. How may I help you?"

"This is Edith Fowler, a patient. I was in several weeks ago and I know it is a long shot but is there anything available for later today or tomorrow?"

"Oh my, love, I doubt it but let me have a quick look. Are you a current patient?"

Edith was pacing frantically back and forth in her flat as she waited. She held the phone to her ear by craning her head to the right and pinning it against her shoulder. She needed to have her hands free to wring them nervously as she paced.

Edith said, "Yes, Edith Fowler."

There was a long pause.

"I'm afraid I don't find that name here dear."

Then it dawned on Edith, she had used her maiden name.

"Sorry, I meant Edith Thatcher. Not used to my married name yet," and she cringed at the lame excuse.

She could hear the rustling and shuffling of papers.

"Ms. Thatcher" she heard the voice say on the other end.

Then she responded audibly, "Yes, I'm here."

"This is your lucky day. There was just a cancellation and you can come in today at 3:00 for an hour."

"My lucky day, indeed," she thought, "If you only knew."

Edith took a long breath and decided.

"That is wonderful, ma'am, I'll be there. Thank you so much."

"Pleasure, Miss," she said, and they both hung up.

Edith needed to hurry to get ready. She took a quick shower and dried her hair and pulled it up in a bun. She pulled out the same outfit she had worn on her first and only other visit to Lunat. She did not have many wardrobe options and she considered that men do not remember what people wear from day to day let alone from week to week. If Lunat were a woman, she would have to find another outfit to wear.

If she was going to make this appointment on time everything would have to work without a glitch.

"Please let the bus be on time," she said as she rushed out onto the street.

It was, and she climbed aboard. Next she hoped for light to reasonably moderate traffic. Maybe it *was* her lucky day because by London's standards this traffic was downright silly; the bus moved forward unimpeded and right on schedule if not a slight bit ahead.

"This is working out," she thought to herself, "how unusual."

She got off of the bus and walked to Lunat's office the same way she had done a few weeks before.

"Ms. Thatcher," Lunat said, "I was expecting you the Thursday next after our last appointment. I was rather looking forward to it and was right disappointed when you did not keep that plan. May I ask why?" Lunat said as Edith entered his office for the second time.

She sat down before answering, and he sensed

something was wrong.

"Has something been wrong, my dear?"

And she recounted it for him. He listened for fifteen minutes without any interruption as she went over the call she got from her husband in Las Vegas while she sat peacefully on the bench by the river after their first appointment. She described her trip to America and her meeting with Mary, and the serendipitous circumstances that led up to it. She described visiting her husband in a dank county jail in Nevada, and how surreal it all was. She told him about the day in court and the judge and the lawyers. And she told him about the devastating accident at the jail. She went into great detail about the anxiety of the wait for news about her husband, and she told him how it felt when she heard that he was dead. She talked about her trip back to London, alone, afraid, and a mess. She talked about how it felt to read the autopsy report for a dead husband. And then she told him about the call she had received from her new dear friend, Mary, and about the letter.

She was surprised when she finished that he had not said a word or uttered a sound. He had hardly moved or fidgeted for that matter. He was engrossed, and it took a second for him to speak even after it was clearly his turn.

"I am so sorry, Edith," he said. "What a terrible time you've been through. How have you coped so far?"

"Funny that you assume I've coped," she said.

"It's not an assumption, Edith. It's a fact. You're here, therefore you have coped. The question pending is how?"

She recognized that he was right; survival equaling coping, and she said, "I have coped on some level. How have I done it you ask? Hmmm, that is a tough one. I suppose by taking it a very little step at a time. I mean at first it was hard to believe – no more than that - it was unbelievable. You hear your husband is dead, at 33, and you only hear it. You don't feel it because it can't be right. I've heard the stories about how people expect their dead loved ones to come home and tell them it was all a joke, to show up at breakfast as if nothing happened. I always thought that was immature drivel. Maybe it is; but it is real. The feeling and expectation, at least, are real. And maybe the slow descent into reality is the psyche's way of cushioning the blow. But that's your field not mine."

Edith paused to reflect and she blew her nose into a tissue she plucked from the box next to her seat. Lunat did not speak so she continued.

"That's what's so disconcerting about this bloody letter. It knocks me back several paces."

"How do you mean?" he asked, mostly to prompt her to continue and to not lose the momentum in her train of thought.

"As things sink in from day to day, and as T.S. does not show up in the morning for breakfast, and as you go to the bank to close accounts, and as you go to the vehicle bureau to transfer a title, or as you go to the landlord to tell them changes are needed, the whole reality of it, well, becomes real. And now, in a bizarre sense, this letter is a temporary resurrection. He still has something to say, and I haven't heard it yet. Does that make him alive again?"

"Of course not, Edith, but I fully understand how it has affected your ability to deal with his death in a linear progression, which, by the way, will never stay on track. There will always be some little thing, sometimes a big thing, here and there which in a sense is a resurrection, a reincarnation of the person you love and the person you miss so

357

dearly. But isn't that the beauty of it in a way? I don't know if you're religious, and it's of no consequence to my point. But religious or not there is a sense of eternal life in what people remember about those who have passed: what they did or what they failed to do as people. There is always an inevitable legacy, which pops up here and there based on the oddest things. The scent of a favorite dish that conjures up a memorable dinner conversation or a romantic encounter or a fight that ended miserably. A certain color of a sunset, a song, a windy day. Who knows? It's always there."

She was crying softly.

"Does that make sense?" Lunat asked.

"Yes, it does." She fell back into her own world for a few precious seconds. "And now I'm left to wonder what T.S.'s legacy is or will be or won't be or how it will be different for different people. Or worst of all I think about and wonder whether it will be small and inconsequential."

He looked at her and waited for more.

"And how this bloody letter will add or detract from it."

Their time was up. Lunat asked her to come back after she read the letter. She promised to think about it, but decided not to commit or settle on an appointment just yet. He shook her hand gently and wished her the best, assuring her that whatever the letter said it would be fine. That there was no outcome that could not be readily handled. She was not convinced.

After she left the office, Lunat looked down at the last note he had written, "She never mentioned the man who her husband killed."

It was raining. She flipped up her umbrella and walked through the rain, directly back to the bus stop. She would not divert her path on this occasion.

Now and again the wind kicked up and blew rain sideways and onto her. She barely felt it.

She closed her umbrella and shook off as much of the moisture as she could before she boarded the bus. Thankfully, there were seats. It was nearing rush hour and traffic would be much heavier now, and it would lengthen the trip considerably from the earlier drive into the appointment. She plunked down in a window seat near the middle of the bus. To avoid casual and unwanted conversation she pulled out her earphones and placed them in each ear. She turned on the music and listened to *Pauvre Type* by Amadou and Mariam. It seemed fitting. It reminded her of how much French she had forgotten.

As the bus rolled slowly through the late afternoon traffic the sun tried to peek through the spotty grey ceiling. They passed through a construction site that slowed them even more. Men with hard hats looked up at the bus, some smoking cigarettes, others leaning lazily on tools and implements. They propped themselves on orange construction vehicles with large red triangular flags hanging off of the machines. The scene passed by her ever so slowly like an artsy Italian film. She listened to the music and absorbed the ordinary surroundings.

The bus passed through a tunnel and everything went black except for the headlights and taillights of the other vehicles inching their way through the tube with the bus. The bus came out on the other side and the sun was again firmly behind a low, thick layer of dark grey.

Edith was tired. She tried to sleep but could not. She tried to rest her eyes, like her father used to tell her to do when she was a little girl and when she could not fall asleep, but she could not rest her eyes; there was no rest. She tried relaxation exercises she had seen on the public television station. They did not work; there was no relaxation. She got a cramp in her calf while doing the exercises; so there was something for the effort.

There was a short break in the traffic and the bus picked up speed. They drove through a park and green trees rushed past her just outside the window. Beyond the trees was a brown stream that came in and out of view as the foliage thinned and thickened. There did not seem to be any current in the stream. The water was dark and still. In the water was a perfect mirror reflection of the trees that grew full on its banks. Edith looked at the reflection and wondered how artists managed to capture the subtleties of the landscape in all its forms and various perspectives.

The bus left the park and entered back into the dense traffic in her neighborhood. She pulled the earphones out of her ears and switched off the music. She was getting close to her stop so she took inventory of her things and got ready to get off of the bus.

As the bus turned left onto the street where her stop was located she got up to move closer to the middle exit. She stood with her handbag clutched firmly under her right arm and held onto the pole by the exit with her left hand. It was still dark and gloomy but it did not appear to be raining. She left her umbrella in her handbag.

Everything on the street was very familiar to her now. There was the apothecary where she would get T.S. aspirin when he had overindulged. There was the record shop where T.S. had bought her the Frank Zappa box set for one of her birthdays; she could not remember exactly which one. There was the coffee shop where she and T.S. would go for cheap tea and free Wi-Fi. There was the crack in the sidewalk where she had tripped and broken her wrist. T.S. cared for her while she only had the use of one hand. It was one of her most tender memories of him.

The bus stopped and she got off. She took a long look down the street, first to the right and then to the left. Everything seemed fairly normal. People walked in and out of the shops, they chatted on their cell phones, and they strolled hand in hand, or arm in arm, or stride for stride.

"Appearances can be very deceiving," she thought. "Something is missing and they don't even know it."

She walked back to her flat. She closed the door behind her and locked it, double checking the latch. She put her handbag down and kicked off her shoes. She sat down on the couch and bent down to rub her feet.

She had put her phone on vibrate while she was in with Lunat and had not yet put it back on the normal ringer. She heard the buzzing in her handbag and reached in to pull out the phone.

There was a text from Mary: "Letter sent by UPS. Delivery scheduled for tomorrow morning your time. Tracking number is YT666669875. Thinking of you. Mary."

Edith typed in "Thanks," and hit reply. She read the text message again and put the phone back in her handbag. Before she did, she put the ringer on silent.

Chapter 35

Edith did not sleep much, so she did not really wake up as much as come out of a weary fog. She sat up and looked at the clock on the night stand. It was 5:45, exactly ten minutes from the last time she had looked and about twenty minutes from the time before that and so on. She was over the waiting game and just decided to give up and get out of bed.

She dragged herself to the kitchen and turned on the flame under the tea kettle filled with water. She went to the cupboard to get out the tea service and placed it on the small dinette table. In not too long a time the kettle whistled, the tea was brewed, and she was having her first cup.

She waited for the sun to come up. Eventually it did. And unlike the day before, this morning was sunny and bright and cheerful. She pulled open the blinds to let the sun shine in.

After her shower, she took her time dressing. She glanced at the clock, and it was now 7:35. She could not remember ever getting an overnight package so she had no idea when to expect it. She didn't have an internet connection in her flat so she could not check the package by its tracking number. She was waiting for it to be a slightly more reasonable hour before she rang up friends with internet connections to ask them to track it for her. Meanwhile, she paced and waited.

She couldn't wait anymore.

She pulled on a sweater and headed out for the coffee shop/tea salon that had free Wi-Fi and at least one computer terminal for public use. The morning air was pleasantly cool, and the sun shone brightly down and was slowly warming things up nicely. She walked past the outdoor flower vendors who were just opening up shop. She passed by the commuters busily and purposefully walking to their offices, or their trains, or their buses. She crossed to the other side of the street so she could stay in the sun. When she got to the internet café she crossed back over and went inside.

Someone was sitting at the public computer so she would have to wait some more. She ordered an Earl Grey tea and sat down to watch it steep. She kept her eye on the computer and on the young man who seemed to be aimlessly surfing for nothing in particular and for everything in general. When she sipped her tea and noticed it was almost drained she decided to intervene.

"Good morning, mate," she said to the young man at the computer keyboard.

"Morning," he said, without as much as looking up.

"I have a small favor to ask," she said, trying to gauge his reaction as she went.

"Yeah, what's that?" he said, again never averting his eyes from the screen.

"I just need to take a quick look to track an important parcel. It won't take but a minute, and you can pop right back on."

He finally looked up at her. He appeared visibly agitated. And without saying a word he got up.

"You'll be quick won't you?" he asked.

"Very, thank you so much," she said, and she replaced him in the seat and typed UPS in the Google search bar. Within a few seconds she had the page where she could plug in the tracking number and derive the current location of her letter and get an estimated delivery time.

She clicked on the "Track Package" icon and typed

in the tracking number: YT666669875.

She read quickly past the pick-up in Las Vegas time and the leave Louisville KY time and the arrival in London time and went straight to the last entry: "On truck for delivery; estimated delivery time today by 3:00 p.m." She looked over at the young man from whom she had borrowed the computer and, satisfied that he was not looking, she hit the "Refresh" button, but the information was the same.

She got up and called over to him, "Thank you, mate, all done here."

He sat back down in silence and resumed his mindless endeavors.

She finished the last speck of tea and put her cup in the plastic tub. She walked back out onto the sunny street. The information she had received was helpful but painfully non-specific. She knew now that her letter was in London, on a truck somewhere, and would be delivered to her flat any time between now and 3:00. She thought about walking about a bit, but decided to head back to her flat and wait it out there.

She walked briskly toward her front door, thinking to herself that another spot of tea might help alleviate the tension.

As she approached her front door she saw something stuck onto it. Her heart began to race and she picked up her pace. She was almost running when she got to the door and tore the sticker from the window and started to read:

"Sorry we missed you. You have a UPS package that requires a signature for delivery. We will make another attempt tomorrow. If you want to make other arrangements, please call…"

She started to cry. She could not possibly wait another day. She was sobbing and her chest was heaving.

"Are you alright, ma'am?" she heard a voice from behind her.

At first she waved the good Samaritan away with a backhanded gesture.

He persisted, "Are you sure you're alright?"

Annoyed, she turned quickly to address the man who would not take no for an answer. Before she could say anything she noticed the brown uniform and the yellow UPS insignia and she cried again – this time with relief.

She was sitting on her couch with the UPS Letter in her hands, which were trembling out of control. She had started to rip it open several times but on each occasion was paralyzed by fear. She had agonized over getting it and now she agonized over seeing it.

She put the UPS envelope down on the coffee table. She walked over to the kitchen and opened the drawer where she kept important papers. She lifted out the letter that she had written to T.S., the one that she never got to deliver, and the one that he would never read; the one she had written in Mary's house while sirens blared outside on the emergency vehicles on the way to the jail where her husband was trapped in the rubble. She pulled her letter to him close to her breast.

All at once she decided. She tucked her letter into her knapsack and put the UPS envelope, unopened, right next to it. She pulled to close the tabs on the top of the sack and double checked to make sure neither envelope could fall out. She opened the front door and checked the temperature with her hand. She decided against the sweater and put the knapsack straps over each shoulder and bounded out the door.

The route was now familiar to her. She sat down at

the bar and put the knapsack between her feet, clutching it between them. She opened the menu. Underneath the large "Shepherd's Place" logo she ran down the list that looked vaguely familiar, after all it had been several weeks.

"Good day, miss," said the barkeep. "What can I get for you?"

"A pint of Olde English and a ham sandwich with chips."

"Right away."

She ate in silence. Nothing around her seemed to matter. Despite the circumstances, she actually enjoyed her lunch. "Odd," she thought.

She arrived at the bench, her bench, near the river just before 1:30. Children were playing on the monkey bars while their mums and nannies chatted nearby with arms waving and bodies swaying. The sun was warming and soothing. She remembered it all, all too well.

The sameness of the day, and the sun, and the bench, and the lunch, and the children, and the mums, and the nannies made it seem alright to open the package now. She picked up her knapsack and pulled out the UPS envelope. She gripped the tab firmly and ripped it open. The paper unzipped at the top and she reached in to pull out a soiled envelope with the words Dear Edith. There was a loose piece of note paper. She read it: "Edith, All the best to you. My heart goes out to you. I miss you, Mary." She smiled as she pictured Mary.

She looked a long time at the hand printed Dear Edith on the envelope. She imagined the pen in his hands. She imagined how his face looked while he took care to print it carefully. She knew that he knew that she abhorred poor penmanship. She smiled as she thought of it.

She carefully broke the seal on the envelope. She took the paper out of the envelope and with great care placed the envelope back into the knapsack. She unfolded the white sheets and started to read:

"Dear Edith,

I hope they find me soon, for our sakes.

My worry right now is that you are worried; my fear right now is that you are afraid; and my pain is that you are suffering. I have put you through so much and now this. God bless it Edith, I am sorry.

I have missed a big part of every part of my life so

far, Edith. I have lived on excuses, plodded along with crutches, and never given much thought about how it impacts the ones I love, and more importantly the few who managed to still love me.

What you deserve is happiness, peace, stability, love. I have provided none of these.

What you have given to me I have not returned.

I may have lost my chance. But you have not.

All I want, whether it is to be with me or not with me, is for you to love life and love living. If I am lucky enough to see you again, I beg for another chance. If I draw dead, then I want you to move forward, to forget the past, and to make a new, beautiful life for yourself.

I am a fool. You are the most beautiful woman I have ever seen or known. Life dealt me a royal flush, and I folded it. I am asking you for a re-deal.

I wish I could muster the strength to write more, but I am growing weak and my thoughts are clouding. I have to finish.

I love you. As hard as it may be for you to believe it, I always have. What I need to do is love myself.

Your loving husband,

t.s."

Edith sat quietly. For a long time. She folded the white paper carefully and placed it back into the dirty envelope with Dear Edith on it. She placed the envelope against her cheek. She put it into the sack and took out the envelope with her letter to T.S. in it. She took that letter out and read it to herself.

Edith stood and picked up her knapsack. She walked toward the river. She took a cigarette lighter from her bag.

Edith took a long breath. She looked up into the clear blue sky. She took the letter she had written to T.S. and held it over the river. She took the lighter and flicked it until a flame came from it. She touched the flame to the top right hand corner of the envelope. It ignited. She held it at the bottom left corner and watched the flame slowly descend on her message, consuming it. She watched the smoke swirl into the heavens. She held onto the letter for as long as she could until to do so any longer would burn her. At the last moment, she let go. And the remnants fell down into the river below. The swift current took away what little that was left.

Edith walked back to the bench, sat and folded her arms. She waited patiently for the sun to set.

She took out her late husband's letter and re-read it. As she was about to put it carefully back into the envelope she found a loose leaf of paper that she had not seen before. She pulled it out. In a different color ink, and in penmanship unbecoming the Brit, it read:

"P.S. Edith: Just in case I am not found alive, I want you to know what happened to me in here. I want you to know that I never gave up fighting with every fiber of my being and soul to get back to you. Whatever caused this explosion did not hurt me badly. From that, I got a few cuts and scrapes but nothing much at all really. My ears hurt and rang from the noise but I was reasonably sure that would pass. The real blow came from a fellow inmate, one who wanted the bottle of water I had. I offered to share it with him, Edith, I swear on my life I did, but he wanted it all. He took a pipe and slammed it into my neck, right into my throat where the Adam's apple sits. His eyes were crazed, like he could not help but attack me for the water that I had. He got my water, Edith, and I couldn't even yell at him while he drank half of it in front of me and then disappeared through a small opening in a far wall. I haven't been able to talk since he hit me and it is harder and harder for me to breathe. I wanted to share my water, not give it all away when it was what I needed to survive."

Epilogue

Patti Berry sat at her kitchen table, sipping coffee and aimlessly turning the pages of the local newspaper. Several weeks had passed since her husband's death. She spent much of her time alone, thinking. She also spent a lot of time looking into the mirror to judge whether her belly was any bigger. Soon enough it would be.

Patti looked at the clock on the coffee maker and folded the paper and placed it neatly on the small table by the phone. As she turned from the table, she saw the beat up white sedan sitting at the curb in front of her house. She peered through the curtains to get a closer look.

Behind the wheel, slightly slumped over, was Jimmy Gatlin. She could not tell if he was asleep, or passed out, or thinking, or dead, or what. She was afraid. She thought about calling the police. She stared out the window and waited for Jimmy to move, or drive off, to do something.

She slipped on a light jacket and opened the front door. She walked slowly down the sidewalk toward the banged up Chevy. She never took her eyes off of the figure in the front seat.

As she got closer, she was able to see into the

passenger side window. On the seat next to Jimmy was a mason jar, with just a little white liquid floating at the bottom. He's drunk, she thought, and she turned about face to head back inside. Before she got very far, she heard his voice, "Mrs. Berry. Mrs. Berry, wait please. I gotta talk to you."

She paused, her arms folded tightly around her midsection. She thought quickly. I can run inside, lock the door and call the police. Instead, she slowly turned around to face Jimmy.

"What is it, Jimmy?" she said. "Why're you sitting out here this morning?"

"I been sittin' out here every mornin' for a week, ma'am," he said. "I just never set this long 'til today."

She thought again about running inside.

She stayed, "That's a little odd, Jimmy, don't you think?"

"Yeah, it is. But I don't mean no harm. I just been waitin' to tell ya somethin' real important, and I ain't been able to bring myself around to it."

Patti looked in each direction down her street to see if anyone was out or around, and she saw no one. Once again she considered making a break to the house, but she did not move.

Patti took a few steps toward Jimmy, who was now out of the car and leaning on the passenger side door. When she was about 10 feet away she stopped. When he started to move toward her, she said "Just stay there Jimmy, if you don't mind. We're plenty close for me to hear what you have to say."

He complied without any protest, and stepped back to lean on the car again. He looked at his feet for a long time. She waited.

"This is really eatin' at me, Mrs. Berry, so I think I'm just gonna go ahead right here and blurt it out."

She did not say anything, but she kept her eyes focused carefully on his. He could not maintain the eye contact. He shook his head ever so slightly and looked back down at the ground. He turned his head away and spat a brown glob on the grass between the sidewalk and the curb.

"Excuse me, ma'am," he said. "I don't usually have to spit when I rub but today I can't seem to keep any spit in my mouth."

She nodded, as if to say she understood. She

waited from him to speak.

Jimmy took a deep breath and, without looking up, started to talk at the ground.

"I shoulda let that preacher have it a few weeks back, ma'am, after he up and went talkin' all about the way that British son of a bitch killed Dan. I'm ashamed to say I just didn't have the balls."

He looked up only for a second to see if his language had offended her. He did not notice any change in her expression or demeanor. He looked quickly back down to the ground.

"I been drinkin' a little bit more than usual since that day at the church. Ya see, I listened to you tell that preacher what for," and he looked up at her with admiration. "But when I got to thinkin' about what all you said, well, I realized you wanted that British guy to suffer in different ways. It seemed like him dyin' right quick wasn't what you was after at all." He spat and went on. "Ya see, I don't think like that, I guess. I'd just as soon kill the son of a bitch and be done with it." He paused and put his hand to his face and rubbed his short beard.

Patti finally spoke to break the silence. "Why is this bothering you so much, Jimmy?"

"That's what I'm aimin' to explain ma'am."

"Ok, Jimmy. Explain."

"Well, Mrs. Berry, do you remember about two, two and a half years ago my cousin got himself arrested for making crystal meth in his garage over on Turkeyfoot Rd.?"

"Not really, Jimmy."

"Well, it don't matter if you remember it or not."

She waited again for him to go on.

"Anyway, he got off easy – first offense and all – and he didn't do no time."

To break another awkward silence Patti said, "And?"

"Well, he and a buddy figured stayin' around here was not very smart and so they bought an old beat up pickup and headed out west. They told everyone they was gonna start fresh and all, stay clean, you know, the regular bull…", and he caught himself before cursing and finished with "bullcrap."

He went on this time without any prodding. "Well, it was bullcrap alright and he gets himself into trouble all the time out there. He's been making meth, robbing convenience stores, and he's in and outta jail like it's the Salvation Army shelter."

"Where is he, Jimmy?" she asked.

"Lately, mostly in Las Vegas."

Her mind started to race.

He continued. "Ma'am, I didn't know how you wanted things. Honest, I didn't. Like I said, it never occurred to me that you wanted that man to stay in jail and think and worry and do all those things you done told the preacher that day."

"Jimmy. What happened?"

"I told my cousin that there was a man in that jail, where he happened to be, that had done a really bad thing to a feller from back here. And I told him if he got the chance he could do a right thing himself for a change. And when that gas line blew out there, well, that give him the chance. With all the chaos and all the confusion he said it was right easy. And he didn't even have to let on that he was doin' it for everyone back here in Bromley. Said he thought it better not to mention that in case the guy survived. But he done it right good, and the

British son of a bitch is dead."

Patti slumped down to the sidewalk and sat down with her head in her hands.

"Ya see, Mrs. Berry, that preacher was full of shit, just like you said he was. God didn't kill that British murderer. I done it, through my cousin."

Patti never looked up. She just sobbed into her hands and mumbled, "Oh my god, oh my god."

Made in the USA
Charleston, SC
03 June 2011